"I WAS TO help him discover his identity," said Jane. "It was exciting, a kind of adventure. Why would he leave without a word?"

Mr. Sharratt nodded sympathetically. "No doubt he remembered who he was, and his first thought was to reach home. Perhaps he will seek you out later."

She brightened at that thought, but remembered what he had left behind. "The snuff box," she exclaimed. "What shall we do with it?"

The lawyer examined the jeweled box carefully. He was about to hand it back when something caught his eye. "Look, Miss Jones, here is a groove! The bottom of the box slides off!"

The thin gold lid came off to reveal a small compartment in the base of the snuff box. In it rested a single sheet of folded paper . . .

Other books by Alice Chetwynd Ley

*A SEASON AT BRIGHTON

*THE TOAST OF THE TOWN

*THE GEORGIAN RAKE

THE MASTER AND THE MAIDEN
(Original title: *Master of Liversedge*)

*THE CLANDESTINE BETROTHAL

*THE COURTING OF JOANNA
(Original title: *The Guinea Stamp*)

Coming soon from Ballantine Books

LETTERS FOR A SPY

TENANT OF CHESDENE MANOR

THE BEAU AND THE BLUESTOCKING

*Published by Ballantine Books

The Jeweled Snuff Box

Alice Chetwynd Ley

BALLANTINE BOOKS • NEW YORK

ISBN 0-345-25809-6-125

Manufactured in the United States of America

First Ballantine Books Edition: April 1974
Second Printing: January 1977

CONTENTS

THE
JEWELED
SNUFF BOX

CHAPTER I

ON THE DARTFORD ROAD

Snow was falling steadily, relentlessly, over the fast darkening landscape; whirling before a keen wind to descend on the stark black branches of the trees and hedges, clothing them in unexpected foliage. The winding road appeared as smooth as a carpet, but the sweating horses, plunging in the soft white mass up to their fetlocks, found the treacherous ruts that lay beneath. In these from time to time they stumbled, recovering themselves and straining onwards, the veins in their necks standing out like thick strands of rope as they pulled the great black coach behind them.

The outside passengers on the London stage shivered, turning up their coat collars and drawing their rugs more closely about them. They looked like grotesque snowmen fashioned by children at play. The coachman, a burly individual in a many-caped driving coat, turned his red, weatherbeaten face towards the guard.

"We can't keep going in this much longer, not nohow," he opined, in a deep voice which carried above the moaning of the wind.

The guard assented, tucking his yard of tin under his arm, the better to slap his hands against his sides in a vain effort to warm them. He thought regretfully of the glass of hot toddy which he might have been enjoying in the tap-room of the Red Lion at that moment, had the coach been running to schedule.

The inside passengers peered anxiously through the windows in the fast gathering dusk. In a little while, it would be dark, and even this diversion would be denied them.

"Reckon it'll keep this up all night," said the man in the buff coat and kersey small clothes. He had the look of a countryman, perhaps a farmer in a prosperous way of business, and the other passengers were prepared to accept his opinion on the weather. One or two of them tut-tutted, and

1

wondered how long it would take to reach Dartford, which was the next stage.

"We've a good eight miles to go yet," he reminded them, pessimistically. "And this is a powerful bad road, even in daylight and fair weather."

The young couple seated next to him, and who appeared to be related to him in some way, exchanged glances. Under cover of the basket which the girl carried, their hands met. They had not long been married, and as far as they were concerned, it was no matter if it snowed all night. They had no complaint to make as long as the concealing darkness permitted them to exchange tendernesses in comparative privacy.

The girl glanced half contemptuously, half pityingly at the young lady in the opposite corner. Three and twenty if she was a day, and a quiet little dowd of a woman with her shabby grey pelisse and plain bonnet with never so much as a bright ribbon trimming. An old maid, thought Matilda, glancing at the ungloved left hand; and likely to remain so. If a girl was not married at one and twenty, she had best give up all hope: Matilda herself was just eighteen. She would be a governess, that one, very like; there was an air of downtrodden Quality that went with the breed. She had never known what it was like to lie close and snug to a man, thought Matilda, edging closer to her husband, to feel the swift rise of passion as his lips took yours, to glory in his strength, and your weakness. At this point in her reflections, she forgot about the young woman in the corner, and became immersed in her own emotions.

Miss Jane Spencer had noticed the glance, and having her fair share of perception, had interpreted it correctly. The young country wife in the opposite seat was pitying her for an old maid. Pity was something she had never sought, refusing herself even the indulgence of her own; yet for a moment, she could not help seeing herself through the girl's eyes, and acknowledging ruefully that hers was not an enviable state.

She found herself wondering what kind of life the others were leading, those who had once been with her at Miss Leasowe's Select Young Ladies' Seminary. Certainly not anything like this, she thought with a wry smile; not jolting along in poorly-sprung stage coaches from one depressing post to another. No, most likely they would by now have had their fill of balls, pretty clothes and elegant company, and be settling down in some comfortable establishment with nothing more arduous expected of them but to sustain the part of a good wife and mother.

Her eyes wavered from Matilda's round healthy face, and fixed themselves absently on the snow drifting past the window, filling the ledges and spattering the glass. Of course, it would have been different if her father had lived. Her life would then have followed more closely the pattern of those others. Strange, she thought, that at one period of our lives we should be so close, young ladies of Quality sharing the same dormitory, the same hopes and fears: and then, only a few short years later, to be as far apart in every particular as were the titled lady and her children's governess.

But it was not for this that she missed her father, not for the ease and comfort he could have brought her, and which now she lacked. Her heart cried out for the affection which had bound the two of them closely together against the vagaries of life, for the sense of having someone who belonged. A picture of him rose suddenly in her mind, clear-cut as though he stood before her in the flesh; his head thrown back in laughter, the keen, hawk-like features bright with the zest of living. Her throat constricted, and tears came into the candid grey eyes.

She blinked them angrily away, inwardly giving herself a shake. He had lived his life gloriously, courageously, wringing a laugh from all his trials, never ceasing to hope, in his own phrase, that presently he would come about. What right, then, had she to betray his memory by indulging in melancholy?

She was awakened from her reverie by the slakening pace of the coach. It came to a standstill, and the travellers eyed each other anxiously. The bluff countryman let down the window, admitting a flurry of snow. He shook himself like a dog, and bawled out "Is aught amiss, driver?"

The guard's red face appeared at the open window.

"We'll have to trouble you to get out and walk up the 'ill, ladies and gennelmen; the beasts bain't equal to it. Mr. Beaver there—" he indicated the front of the coach with a jerk of his thumb—"says we can't go much farther in this. There's an inn of sorts at the top o' the rise, and we be thinking it may be best to seek shelter there for the night, and go on in the mornin'."

There was an outcry at this.

"Me darter's meeting me at Dartford," whined a wizened

old woman in a rusty black cloak, who sat beside Jane Spencer. "She'll be rare put about if I bain't there."

"Can't be 'elped, Ma," returned the guard, putting a strong hand under her arm to assist her to alight. "Darters or no darters, we don't go no farther till daybreak—if so be as we can manage to get through then."

The farmer had jumped down after the old woman, and took a long, searching look at the sky.

"Full of it," was his comment. "But it don't generally lie long this time o'year—thaw might set in tomorrow."

The coachman was of a less optimistic turn of mind; the two argued the point while the outside passengers climbed down from their perch, and, after exchanging a few sentences with the disputants, set off at a smart pace up the hill. Matilda and her husband followed the farmer from the coach, and now stood huddled together, waiting until their relative should be pleased to make a move. This he did at last, going up to the old woman and asking if he might carry her basket for her. As it was nearly as big as herself, she relinquished it thankfully; and he fell into step beside her, chattering away in his cheerful country burr. Matilda and her husband, who appeared to have as much idea of what they were about as two sleep-walkers, linked arms and followed in their relative's wake.

Jane Spencer had been the last to alight from the coach, and was now left to walk alone. The chill wind cut through her thin pelisse like a knife, and she drew close in to the hedge in the vain hope of finding more shelter. She had to pick her way with care, for here was a ditch partly submerged in snow, and an incautious step might plunge her into it. After a few yards, she decided wryly that perhaps it would make little difference, after all; the snow reached almost to the top of her half-boots, and already a damp, clammy ring had formed between boot and stocking. She glanced after the men of the party, envying them the boots which reached to the top of their calves, and their warm topcoats. True, it was not the mode for ladies to go warmly clad; but Jane Spencer's garments were, by reason of age, even lighter than fashion demanded.

She shivered, head bent against the driving snow, eyes straining to make out the line of the ditch as she trudged onwards. Her progress was not rapid; the snow clung like lead weights to her feet. The distance between herself and the others increased.

She had reached a point about halfway up the hill, when suddenly she halted in her tracks, her blood chilling from other cause than the weather. An icy inward chill this, seizing her heart in an iron grip and momentarily robbing her of the power of movement. She stood as one turned to stone, her hand coming up to her mouth in an instinctive gesture of terror.

A little way ahead of her, sprawled in the ditch and half covered by snow, lay what appeared from this distance to be a body.

Almost she cried out, but an inherent dislike of making a scene prevented her. It was that eerie time of day when familiar objects take on an unfamiliar look. Perhaps she told herself, in an effort to be rational, this might prove to be only a discarded scarecrow. How humiliating to have summoned the others if it should be so! She must first approach more closely, and make quite sure what the object really was.

Such a decision was easy to make, but not so simple to put into effect. Reluctance held back every nerve in her body. By a supreme effort of will, she at last forced herself onwards, her dragging feet carrying her inexorably towards the ominous bundle in the ditch. She drew level, and timorously stooped over it, her eyes straining through the fading light. With difficulty she made out a huddle of dark garments, and then, clearly outlined against the snow, an outflung human hand.

Involuntarily, she let out a little scream.

The others turned at the sound, and the men came running towards her.

"What's amiss?" shouted the farmer.

For answer she pointed with a shaking finger to the crumpled body in the ditch. For a moment, speech had deserted her.

"Good God, it's a corpse!" gasped the farmer. "Hey, there, stop the coachman, some of you, and bring a lantern!"

Two of the outside passengers ran to do his bidding. The farmer and the other men stooped over the body, and lifted it into the road.

"What's toward?" panted the guard, running towards them with a lantern in his hand. At sight of the burden the two men were carrying, he let out an exclamation.

"Just set that down 'ere," directed the farmer, "and we'll see if the poor devil's got any life left in 'im. Young lady found 'un in the ditch," he explained tersely.

The guard obeyed, and by the flickering light of the lantern Jane saw a pale, dark-browed face with an ugly bruise over one temple. The farmer bent over the body, and made a brief examination. He straightened up.

"He lives," he said. "Looks as if he's been set upon and robbed, by the state of his clothes. He don't seem to be wounded, though. We'd best carry 'im to the coach. You take 'is head, Jem—" this to his son, who had arrived with the others, leaving Matilda and the old woman standing some distance off in the middle of the road. "Steady now, lad; don't want to go jolting the poor fellow about more'n we can help."

Between them they heaved the body up and bore it, not without some difficulty, to the waiting coach. The guard seized the lantern, and was about to follow them; but as he did so, Jane caught sight of something glinting in the ditch.

"Stay just a moment," she commanded. The man brought his light over to the spot where she was standing, and she stooped to put out her hand to the object she had espied. Her groping fingers closed round something square and hard. She seized it and raised it to the light, brushing the loose snow away from its surface.

It was a jewelled snuff box.

The guard whistled.

"Gold and precious stones," he said, peering closely at the box. "Worth any amount, I'll be bound. Reckon it must 'ave fallen into the ditch when the poor chap was set upon, and that's how the thief came to miss it. Queer place, though, for footpads or highwaymen, with the inn just at the top of the rise—still, no telling where you'll be falling foul o' them gentry. You'd best have a care of it, ma'am; I should put it out of sight."

Jane assented, tucking the box into her reticule, and together she and the guard followed the rest of the party.

They had not far to go before they came to the small inn of which the coachman had spoken. It was an old building with a thatched roof and latticed windows; over the low entrance door swung an unpretentious, snow-covered sign 'The Three Tuns'. Obviously this was no posting house, but a wayside inn catering only for the casual traveller. Nevertheless, a warm red light shone from the curtained window of the coffee-room, and the weary travellers heaved a sigh of relief at the prospect of a meal and a cheerful fire to sit by.

The landlord of the inn was a typical Boniface, round of

face and form, but his wife was altogether another matter, and it was soon plain to see who ruled the affairs of the Three Tuns. Under her disapproving eye, the passengers from the stage coach crowded into the coffee-room, drawn to the fireside as moths to a candle flame. The coachman and the guard lingered in the hall to explain their predicament.

When she had heard them out in a silence that boded no good, the landlady gave them to understand that they must not expect too high a standard of hospitality at the Three Tuns. She pointed out forcibly that there were only two vacant bedchambers at the inn, and those but small. Moreover, she had not been prepared to find supper for ten extra persons, and all the serving maids but one had gone home early because of the weather. When she was made to understand that she was also expected to accommodate an unconscious man who had been found by the wayside, her indignation waxed so strong that it drew Jane forth from the coffee-room.

"I'll have no such person in here!" exclaimed the landlady emphatically. "Most like he was blind drunk, and fell off his horse on the way home!" .

"Nay, now, ma'am," replied the coachman, as though he were gentling a restive mare, "I tell you the poor fellow's been set on and robbed. All his pockets turned out as clean as a whistle—not a penny piece could we find on him, nor so much as a letter."

"And if that's the case, how am I to be paid for my trouble, I'd like to know?" asked the irate landlady.

"Why, 'e's a man of consequence, as anyone may see from his clothes," replied the man, nothing daunted. "When he comes to 'e'll give you 'is name, and all will be well, you'll see."

"I certainly hope so," retorted the she-dragon, with a toss of her head. She did not sound convinced.

"You surely cannot mean to refuse shelter to an unconscious man?" asked Jane incredulously. "As far as the account is concerned, I can assure you that you need have no fears; this box was found close by his side. You may see for yourself that it is very valuable."

She had drawn the snuff box from her reticule as she spoke, and now placed it in the woman's hand. The landlady, who had been surveying Jane contemptuously with arms akimbo while she listened impatiently to her, hastened to take the box, and studied it attentively. Her sharp face cleared.

"Ay, this'll be worth a pretty penny, right enough. Those are rubies and emeralds, I reckon. I don't know as 'ow you're the best person to have a charge of it, a valuable piece like that."

Miss Spencer's shabby figure seemed to grow inches taller at this remark; but she made no reply, contenting herself with a speaking glance.

"No offence meant, I'm sure!" said the landlady hastily, handing back the box. "Very well then, you may bring him in. Best put 'im on the sofa in the parlour till he comes round—it'll be quieter in there. But it's to be hoped 'e needs no nursing, for I shan't have time to see to it, and so I tell you?"

"Is there any chance of getting a doctor to him?" asked Jane.

The woman shook her head. "Nearest one's five mile away, and even if anyone could get through to him, he wouldn't turn out on a night like this, not for King George hisself! Still, the man bain't wounded, so they say; very like he'll come to in a bit, and be none the worse. And now I must bustle about a bit—all them beds to see to, and a meal to be got!"

Muttering to herself, she made off down the passage in the direction of the kitchen.

The coachman and the guard called the farmer out of the coffee-room to assist them in conveying the injured man within doors. Jane lingered uncertainly in the hall. She had the habit of making herself useful, and though there seemed little she could do in this instance, she was willing to help if she had it in her power.

The men soon returned with their burden, puffing a little under his weight. The party left the fire in the coffee-room for a moment to gaze curiously at the unconscious man.

"Big feller, bain't he,?" cackled the old woman. "Nigh on six feet, I'll be bound."

" 'E looks a well-breeched cove," remarked one of the outside passengers. "Enough capes on his greatcoat for a Mail coachman!"

The others laughed at this, for the dandyism of the drivers of His Majesty's Mail coaches was notorious.

"You bringin' 'im in here, friend?" asked one of the other men, making way for the bearers to enter.

"No, no, don't put yourselves about," answered the coachman. "The landlady's orders was to put 'im in the parlour—best obey the missus, eh?"

The men guffawed, and drifted back to the fire, where the old woman and Matilda had returned some minutes since.

Jane alone followed the men into the parlour, and watched while they deposited the unconscious man gently on the sofa by the fire. This done, they stood looking down at him for a moment.

"Wonder who he is?" said the farmer.

The coachman scratched his head. "No knowing. That chap was right when he said that he was a well-breeched 'un, though. Look at that silk westkit; his coat's made from a rare bit o' cloth, too, and as for his boots—I reckin it took more than blacking to put a shine like that on 'em!"

The others agreed.

"What's to be done with 'un?" asked the farmer. "P'raps a nip o' brandy might bring 'un to. I disremember when I've seen a cove so flat out with nobbut a bump on the 'ead."

"No," interposed Jane quickly, with all the firmness at her command. "Not spirits, I beg! There is no saying what internal injuries he may have. Perhaps we may judge better of that when he recovers consciousness. I think it may possibly be of some benefit to bathe his head, however. I'll see what can be done."

She quitted the room to brave the terrors of requesting the landlady to supply her with a basin and linen for this purpose. It seemed that no one else was prepared to bother themselves any further with the sufferer. The rest of the party were toasting themselves round the fire and awaiting their supper; the farmer joined them, after remarking that no doubt the poor fellow would do well enough presently. The coachman and guard had already left the room to see to the stabling of the horses, so that when Jane finally returned to the parlour bearing the articles she had gone in search of, she found the injured man alone in the room.

While she was performing her office of mercy, she had the opportunity to study him at leisure. He was a man of not more than seven and twenty, she decided, though perhaps in his present state he might look younger than was actually the fact. In some vague way, he reminded her of her father; was it that the colouring was the same, or was it the slightly aquiline sweep of the nose, and the heavy black brows? A lock of thick, dark hair fell across the wet cloth which she had placed on his forehead. His face was pale, and wore the helpless, appealing look of a sleeping child. Jane's heart stirred with compassion.

Even as she looked down at him, he opened blank, uncomprehending eyes.

"Do you feel better now?" she asked softly.

He continued to stare at her in silence, as though he had not heard. She had quite decided that he was not sufficiently conscious to understand her, when a reply came falteringly from his lips.

"I feel vilely!"

The words came up to her as though from the bottom of a well.

"Is it your head?"

He tried to nod, and winced at the effort. The eyes cleared a little.

"Where am I?"

Jane took the cloth from his head, and wrung it out again in the basin before replying.

"You are at an inn upon the road to Dartford," she said quietly, replacing the cloth on his forehead. "You have had an accident. But it is better that you do not trouble yourself over that just now. Try to sleep. Are you thirsty?"

Once again the faint motion of assent. Jane raised his head slightly, and held a tankard of water to his lips. He drank deeply.

The eyes filmed over again as she gently lowered his head. For a moment, he kept them fixed on the fire in an unseeing start; then the lids flickered, drooped, and remained shut.

For some time afterwards, Jane stood there, looking down at him without moving. After a while, she noticed his chest rising and falling in an easy rhythm, and realised that he slept.

CHAPTER II

DILEMMA AT DAYBREAK

THE HARSH rattle of curtain rings recalled Jane from slumber. She opened her eyes, and for a moment or two could not recollect where she was. Her body felt cramped and uncomfortable. She looked about her, and saw that she was in an armchair in the coffee-room of the inn. The cheerful fire of the previous night had degenerated into a powdery mass of grey-white ash, and the room was cold. A pale grey light filtered in through the window.

She shivered, and her eye fell upon a dark figure outlined against the window.

"In God's name where is this place? What am I doing here?"

The voice was deep, pleasantly modulated, though somewhat imperious in its anxiety.

She peered again, recognising the unknown man who had been rescued on the preceding evening. She pushed herself upright in her chair, wincing as the blood returned to her cramped limbs.

"This is an inn upon the road to Dartford," she replied, "by name the Three Tuns."

He came nearer, looking down at her with his heavy dark brows drawn down in a perplexed frown.

"But what am I doing in an inn on the road to Dartford?"

"You have had an accident, sir," said Jane, rising stiffly. "You were found by the roadside yesterday evening, and brought here."

"An accident?"

His tone was incredulous. Jane surmised that he must still be suffering some shock, and spoke in a calm, matter of fact way, hoping to allay his natural alarm.

"We judged that you had been set upon and robbed; we could find no papers or other possessions upon you, and you

11

were unconscious. There was no sign of injury, however, except for a great bruise on your head."

"My head! So that is why it feels sore this morning!"

He grimaced ruefully as he fingered the bruise. It had diminished somewhat overnight, but what it had lost in size it had gained in colour.

"It was not possible to bring a doctor to you, owing to the snow. I trust you have taken no lasting hurt, sir. How do you find yourself this morning?"

"Oh, I am well enough, I thank you, though a trifle sharp-set, I must confess."

"That is understandable," said Jane. "To my certain knowledge, you've not broken your fast for twelve hours. I'll go and see if there is anyone astir to provide you with breakfast."

She turned towards the door, but he put out a hand to detain her.

"No, stay: that can wait. There are things I must know, first."

She paused, and stood waiting for him to continue. He seemed in no hurry to begin, brooding with down-drawn brows and a worried expression.

"You are no servant," he said at last, looking up quickly. "Finding you here, I thought you must be; but your voice and manner—"

"I am one of a party of stage passengers who were obliged to put up here for the night because of the severe weather. It was we who found you by the wayside."

"The common stage? You?"

Abstraction, perhaps, made him less tactful than he would otherwise have been. The dim light covered Jane's slight embarrassment.

"It is my usual mode of travel," she answered simply. He made no reply. When he spoke again, it was on a different subject.

"Are there no beds in this inn? How comes it that I awake to find myself on a sofa in what I suppose must be the parlour, and I find you taking your repose in a chair? 'Pon my soul, mine host must have a very poor notion of hospitality! Wait until I see the fellow!"

"It was very difficult for the landlady," replied Jane. "This is only a small wayside inn, you see, not a regular posting-house. There are but two bedchambers, and we were eight persons on the stage coach, excluding the driver and guard.

You were brought in unconscious, as I said, and lain upon the sofa. Later, you recovered consciousness, and immediately fell into a deep, health-giving sleep. I thought it best—that is, we did not care to disturb you."

"And you?"

Jane hesitated. "I do not care for sharing a bedchamber with females unknown to me. I chose to remain in here."

He gave her a shrewd look.

"There was a basin of water and linen by my side when I woke," he said. "I collect that someone had been bathing my head."

"Well, yes," admitted Jane diffidently. "The landlady was very occupied in the kitchen—I offered my services."

"And then remained here all night in case I should have need of your nursing?" he asked shrewdly.

She nodded. "That did come into it. But indeed, I have the strongest dislike of shared rooms."

A brief smile lightened his sombre face.

"You do not choose to admit it, but I see that I am in your debt. I am very grateful, madam."

She forced a little laugh; she was unused to gratitude, and it embarrassed her.

"It was nothing sir. Anyone might have done as much."

"But no one else did. Moreover, you have sacrificed your night's rest for me. May I not know to whom I owe so much?"

Jane's discomfiture increased, and she avoided his glance.

"My name is Jane Spencer, sir."

He bowed, but to her surprise offered no name in exchange for hers. He fell silent. The keen, alert look left his eyes, and his dark brows came down in a heavy, brooding frown.

Jane saw that he had for the moment forgotten her presence, and she rose quietly with the intention of seeing if there was anyone yet astir in the kitchen. Outside the window, the light was strengthening. The kitchenmaid, at all events, must soon be up and doing.

She was almost to the door when he seemed to become aware of her again. She halted as he spoke.

"This is an odd tale!" he burst out. "For the life of me, I cannot understand it! I have no recollection of being upon the Dartford road, nor of anything that happened there to put me in the sorry plight in which you found me."

"That isn't surprising, sir," replied Jane, reasonably. "You have suffered a shock, and must expect to be in some mental confusion just at first."

"Yes, but—"

He broke off, pondering.

"Where is this place—the spot where you found me, I mean?"

"I should say it was some two hundred yards distant from this inn," replied Jane. "It was halfway up the hill which leads here."

She shivered a little, recalling her fright of yesterday. The man did not notice, too taken up with his own thoughts, which did not seem to be of the happiest.

"That seems an odd spot for a highwayman to choose," he said, frowning again. "Unless, of course, the people here are in league with him."

"Exactly the opinion of the guard of my stage!" exclaimed Jane. "That is to say, he thought it an odd place for a highwayman to lurk. He mentioned no suspicion of the other matter."

"What is your opinion?"

Jane frowned, considering.

"I do not credit it," she said, at last. "After all, I have been here at hand all night, and have heard nothing untoward. Surely these gentry come and go at night?"

He nodded. "One supposes so. Well, we must keep our eyes peeled for any indication of that sort. But I cannot hope to achieve much in the way of detection while I am in the dark as to what really happened to me."

He relapsed into thought once more.

"Was there any conveyance—or a horse—found by me?" he asked suddenly.

Jane shook her head.

"Nothing? Then I must have been on foot." He turned this over in his mind for a few minutes, then exclaimed, "On foot! And in such weather! I could not have come far."

She stared at him. "But surely—"

"Tell me, Miss Spencer," he interposed, ignoring her interjection, "did the people here appear to know me?"

"Know you?" asked Jane, puzzled. "No, they had no notion who you could be. In fact—"

She had been about to say that the landlady was reluctant to admit him, but changed her mind in time. Such news would not make pleasant hearing, and could serve no useful purpose.

He did not notice her unfinished speech, but lapsed into a fit of abstraction. A long silence fell over the room, broken only by the ticking of the clock on the mantelshelf. Jane lingered uncertainly by the door, not knowing whether to go or stay. At length, she crossed over to the window to look out. It was no longer snowing, and a pale sun was struggling to pierce the watery sky.

"I believe it has begun to thaw in the night," said Jane, with a desire to make conversation. From the expression on the man's face, she feared that his thoughts could not be pleasant company. "I do hope it may be so; we cannot look to find much comfort here, and, to speak the truth, the landlady's manner left much to be desired."

He made no answer.

"I suppose you may at least be able to hire a horse here," she continued, in an attempt to draw him out of his abstraction. "Have you far to go to your home, sir?"

"I do not know," he answered, in a tone of great despondency.

She turned and looked at him in surprise. All at once, he went striding restlessly up and down the room.

"That is what I have been trying to find out all this time!" he said, with a wild look. "I have been trying to remember—remember where I live, where I was going, what happened. I find that I can recollect none of these things, not even—"

He broke off, and clapped his hands to his head.

"Good God, it isn't possible!"

She was a little alarmed by his manner, but tried to keep her voice even as she asked, "What is not possible, sir?"

He wheeled on her, his face haggard.

"Such things cannot happen! Indeed, if I tell you, you will think me mad!"

He paused, and made a visible effort to control himself. When he spoke again his tone was quieter.

"Miss Spencer, I cannot even remember my own name."

CHAPTER III

A BARGAIN IS STRUCK

SHE STARTED involuntarily.

"You see!" he cried. "You do think me mad!"

"Not at all." She put a restraining hand upon his arm, drawing him down into a chair. "You must remember that you have had a shock, sir. Such things may cause some odd results, but for a time only. A few more hours, and you will recollect everything."

He put a hand over her wrist, as though seeking support.

"You may be right—you must be right! But suppose it is not hours, but days—even weeks—before I recover my memory? What am I to do meanwhile, with no money in my pockets, nothing to tell me who I am—not knowing where to go?"

"I wish you will not worry," said Jane, firmly. "I am convinced that you will recollect these things in time; but worry is the last thing that will help you to a speedy recovery."

"You are right," he said, releasing her wrist. "Forgive my sudden outburst—perhaps I do need food, after all. But I think you said that there is a crowd of people in this inn—how am I to avoid them? For I never felt less like company, and depend upon it, if they get wind of my state, they will stare at me as though I were some freak from Astley's circus!"

"Do not concern yourself on that score. I fancy I can persuade the landlord's wife to serve you with some breakfast in the parlour," said Jane, moving towards the door.

"I thrust you will honour me with your company?" he asked, rising to his feet.

Jane coloured a little, "I do not know—that is to say—"

"You are thinking that it would not be proper," he said, eyeing her shrewdly.

"Perhaps it is wrong of me to ask it, but I implore you, Miss Spencer, not to leave me to myself at the present time.

17

I cannot explain to you how I feel—it is like some ghastly nightmare—as though I had suddenly found myself completely alone in an alien world. You are my only link with reality until I recover my memory."

"Of course I understand," said Jane softly. "I won't leave you, I promise—or, at least, no longer than it takes to arrange matters with the landlady."

He gave her a grateful glance, then passed his hand thoughtfully over his chin.

"Perhaps, after all, I'd better interview yon dragon of a woman myself," he said, with a faint smile. "I am in no case to breakfast with a lady until I have managed to rid myself of this incipient beard."

It was the first remark he had made which showed a disposition to take the situation lightly. Jane sighed with relief. He was indeed in a most awkward predicament, but she felt assured that time would make all come right. It was unfortunate that there had been no possibility of bringing a doctor to him last night. He looked far from well; signs of strain showed round his eyes and in his pallid cheeks, while his manner varied between deep depression and wildness.

"I should think the landlord would be more to the purpose," she answered. "Besides, he is a more easy person than his wife. Shall I send him to you in the parlour? I advise you to retire there if you wish to avoid my fellow passengers, for they must soon be astir."

He hesitated. "It is infamous that you should have to wait on me!"

Jane smiled. "Think no more of it. I am quite used to be busy, and am only too glad if I may be of assistance."

"You are an angel!" he said impetuously.

She coloured, and whisked quickly from the room.

For some little time now, she had heard vague sounds of activity about the inn, and guessed that the household was astir. She found the landlady in the kitchen, busy rating the kitchenmaid for not pulling the fire up faster. Jane earned the girl's gratitude by interrupting her mistress's homily to inquire if the unknown gentleman could be served with breakfast in the parlour. She explained that he was feeling much better this morning, but that his head ached vilely, and he preferred to take his meal alone.

"Did he say who he was, ma'am?" asked the woman sharply.

"I did not make it my business to inquire," replied Jane coldly, for she found the woman impertinent and disobliging.

"Oh, well, if it's breakfast in the parlour 'e wants, 'e must be Quality, and can pay for it," retorted the landlady, and she promised to see to the matter at once.

Jane then left the kitchen to seek the bedchamber where the women of the party had slept, in order to make her toilet. Here she was bombarded with questions concerning the unknown man. How did he do this morning? What had befallen him to bring him to the plight in which he had been found yesterday? Who was he? To all of these she replied patiently that the gentleman was not yet quite himself, still a little confused, and that the kindest thing would be not to tease him with inquiries. She repeated these answers presently to the male passengers whom she encountered on her way downstairs again to the parlour.

She entered the room to find a cheerful fire burning and a cloth spread on the round polished table, laid with everything needful for a hearty breakfast. Her companion being absent, she did not immediately sit down, but went over to the window and stood looking out. The snow was fast deteriorating into slush, and the dripping trees and hedges presented a forlorn appearance. Still, no doubt it would be possible to continue on their journey, even though the going would be sufficiently difficult for the horses, and very dirty.

The door opened, and the man entered, looking more at ease than formerly. He was freshly shaven, and had made shift to brush his thick dark hair and his clothes, so that his appearance was now more that of a gentleman of fashion. He greeted Jane with a smile, begging her to be seated; and after having in vain tried to persuade her to partake of a slice of beef, fell to with a hearty appetite, leaving her to the rolls and coffee which she evidently preferred.

For some time, conversation languished. At last, the man pushed away his plate.

"I must confess to feeling much more myself," he said, smiling. "But it perplexes me to know how I am to pay for all this."

"It is a difficult business," agreed Jane. "You still cannot recall, then, what happened, or who you are?"

He shook his head despondently. "If I could give myself a name, no doubt mine host would be content to leave the reckoning to my own good time. But who in his senses would allow credit to a nameless man?"

All the cheerfulness which Jane had noted with pleasure before the meal, seemed to have deserted him now. It crossed her mind that these alternating moods of hope and despair, combined with his loss of memory, were signs that he was not as perfectly in health as he thought himself. There could be no doubt that he ought to see a doctor. She said as much to him.

"I tell you that I feel quite myself," he answered vigorously. "But you must surely see that when a fellow can't remember his own name, he is bound to feel a trifle hipped! I want no medico mauling me about, cupping me and Lord knows what besides! No, I am of your opinion when you say that everything will come back to me in time. But, Good God, I haven't much time!"

Jane knew better than to argue with a man whom she was convinced was sick, no matter what he himself might say. She did wish, though, that there was some way of helping him to recover his memory. She suddenly bethought her of the snuff box, and produced it from her reticule with an excited little exclamation.

"There is this, sir; I found it lying by your side in the ditch."

He took it eagerly, and flicked open the lid. He evidently did not find what he sought there, however, for his face dropped. He turned the box over in his hand dispiritedly.

"It tells me nothing. One would imagine that it might touch off some spring of memory, but no!"

He put it down on the table with a dejected air.

"And there is not even an initial on the thing to aid me!"

He had plunged once again into melancholy. Jane, too, felt disappointed, but she smiled reassuringly.

"I am convinced that you will remember in time," she said. "Meanwhile, might you not persuade the landlord to accept this box as surety for your debt?"

His face lit up. "Yes, of course! How clever of you!"

Then he grew downcast as suddenly.

"But what am I to do then, without a penny in my pocket! I cannot remain here indefinitely, waiting for my memory to return. Even though the box might be valuable enough to cover a protracted stay, the inactivity would drive me mad! I must set about doing something to find out who I am!"

Jane could sympathise with these feelings. She remained silent for a moment, puzzling her wits for a way out of his difficulty.

"I have it!" she exclaimed suddenly. "Why do you not come with me to London to see my lawyer? I had the intention of paying him a visit, and moreover there is a vacant seat in the coach."

"A lawyer," he said, consideringly. "Yes, he might indeed be able to assist me to discover my identity. But there is my shot here at the inn, the coach fare and the lawyer's fee—how in the name of thunder can I raise the wind? I might perhaps be able to borrow something on this box at a pawn shop," he concluded, lifting the box from the table and inspecting it once more.

"You would not be paid a quarter of its value!" declared Jane vigorously. "And, for all you may know, it may be the one thing you would be most reluctant to part with. No, I have another idea—though I do not know—"

Here she paused, and looked uncomfortable. She was silent for so long that at last he burst out impatiently, "Do you not mean to tell me what it is?"

"It is this," she said, slowly and with some diffidence; "that you should allow me to be your banker. I fear I have not a great deal about me—" she coloured at this point, for she felt all the impropriety of discussing her finances with a stranger—"but I have sufficient to settle your small affairs; and you can easily reimburse me when you have control of your own means."

He burst out indignantly at this, horrified at the notion of being in debt to a woman, and to one, moreover, who obviously was not too affluent. For the first time, he studied her closely, noting the shabby garments, the many little things that told of straitened means. He observed too, the serious grey eyes, the richly coloured hair that was too severely dressed. She was evidently a gentlewoman, but it was equally plain to see that she had come down in the world. And yet she was prepared to share the little she had with a man of whom she knew nothing. His glance softened.

"You are too generous, Miss Spencer," he said. "For all you can know, I may be a thief, or—or a murderer."

"I think better of my judgement of human nature sir," she returned, with a smile that transformed the serious face. "But are we agreed?"

He hesitated.

"How do we know that I am in a position to repay you?" he asked gloomily.

"Oh, come!" said Jane, in a rallying tone. "You should

have heard the coachman and the guard yesterday evening on that subject."

She gave a spirited rendering of the remarks that had been passed concerning the unknown's garments. She had quite a turn for mimicry, and managed to raise a laugh from her companion.

"So you see, it is quite settled that you are a gentleman of fortune, sir; that being so, I shall be obliged to charge interest."

This time he laughed heartily.

"Usurer! Who would think, to look at you, that you were possessed of such a grasping nature? But I agree to your plan on one condition only."

"And that is—?"

"That you accept this box as surety for my debts. No, do not refuse me—" as she shook her head, and pushed the box away "—I am adamant on this point. If you won't accept my terms, I shall refuse your offer, and raise what I can on the box in the nearest pawn shop."

"That would be a pity," said Jane, with a smile. "You force me to accept."

"Excellent. Let us shake hands on our bargain."

He extended a hand, and after a second's hesitation, she placed hers within it. Swiftly, he carried it to his lips.

"I am your debtor, Miss Spencer, in every way."

She coloured a little at the unaccustomed salute. He was faintly amused. It crossed his mind that the women he was used to meet were not always as modest as this young lady. He liked her the better for it. He gently released her hand.

Jane involuntarily placed her fingers over the spot where his lips had rested. The movement brought her hands into contact with the snuff box. To cover her confusion, she picked it up, and made some affair of placing it safely in her reticule.

She was still at this task when the serving-maid came to clear away the dishes. The girl's presence put an end to further conversation, and Jane quickly excused herself, quitting the room with the ostensible reason of inquiring as to the likelihood of the stage coach continuing on its way to London; but in reality so that she might cool her cheeks.

Left to himself, the man rose from his chair with a quick, impatient movement, and stood before the fire, gazing into its red heart with brooding, perplexed eyes.

CHAPTER IV

THE HISTORY OF JANE SPENCER

By the time they left Dartford, they had the inside of the coach to themselves. Jane's companion had maintained a brooding silence for the greater part of the journey, answering the curious inquiries of his fellow passengers as briefly as the barest civility would allow. When the last of them had descended outside the Red Lion, and the coach once more rattled over the cobbles on its way to London, he heaved a sigh of relief.

"Thank Heavens they have gone!" he exclaimed, turning to Jane. "Another few miles of their questioning, and I believe I should have assaulted one of them!"

She laughed, and he noticed how much younger she appeared when her face was animated. That bonnet she was wearing was a sorry mistake; her whole appearance was too subdued for a female of her years. Pinched in the pocket, obviously, he thought, covertly studying the shabby pelisse; but surely he was right in thinking that she made a deliberate effort to submerge her looks and personality? Most women sought to enhance such looks as they had; why was this one set on another course? For the first time, he forgot his own weighty problem in curiosity concerning this girl who had proved such a friend in need.

"Tell me about yourself," he urged.

Jane looked surprised. It was an odd request for a comparative stranger to make, but then everything connected with her present adventure was unusual. And was he so much of a stranger, after all? She felt as if she had known him all her life. She laughed a trifle self-consciously.

"There is nothing worth the telling, sir."

"That I do not believe. But I see that I must cross-question you; you are evidently incurably modest."

He saw that she looked a little uncomfortable, and was instantly contrite.

"I beg your pardon: no doubt you think me impertinent."

"No, I assure you," protested Jane.

"Our association has been so very unusual that I am forgetting the usual rules of conduct. I was thinking—selfishly —that if you were to tell me something of your own life, it would prevent me from brooding over my lack of ability to recall mine."

She realised that, and decided to humour him.

"What shall I tell you?" she asked, smiling.

"About your family, where you live, your opinions on the novels of Mrs. Radcliffe, the voice of Mrs. Billington, and the present peace with Boney—oh, everything and anything! I feel I want to know you through and through—that there is something stable in my world!"

He said this half lightly, half wildly, so that she was puzzled to interpret his mood aright. One thing caught her attention, however.

"Your recollection of the events in the world about you seems to be sufficiently sound, sir," she remarked.

"By Jove, so it does!"

His manner brightened at once. He paused to consider. At length, he shook his head.

"I find I can name you all the foremost statesmen of the day, without being able to, say whether any one of them is a personal friend. My own name remains as much a mystery to me as before. But still, there must be hope, if recollection can go as far as this!"

"Have I not been telling you so since early this morning?" said Jane, with a teasing smile.

"So at least you are like other women in that!" he retorted.

"In what, sir?"

"The sex as a whole cannot refrain from saying 'I told you so'. You spoke very much as a sister would."

"You would appear to be very knowledgeable," replied Jane demurely; then, her expression altering, "Have you a sister?"

The animation left his face. "I do not know," he said, in a hopeless tone.

"Then we will speak of my affairs," said Jane, firmly. She was determined that he should not be allowed to brood. "What did you ask me? Oh, yes, I recollect! What do I think of the present peace—well, sir, I fear that I'm convinced it cannot last. My father once said that there could be no peace with Napoleon, that he was possessed of a thirst for power that could never be assuaged; our only hope lay in opposing him to the utmost."

"I am of a like mind," he replied, rousing a little. "Addington and his followers are mutton-heads! But you mentioned your father—"

He broke off, not caring to ask a direct question.

"My father is dead," replied Jane quietly. "He was a Naval man, and was killed in the action off Cape St. Vincent five years ago."

There was no self-pity in her even tone, yet in some indefinable way the man realised the depth of her grief.

"I am sorry."

It was an inadequate remark, he knew; but there was nothing he could find to say that would in any way convey his very real sense of sharing in the sorrows of this girl whom he had known only a few hours.

"And your mother?" he asked gently, after a pause.

"She died when I was but a baby. I do not remember her."

He was silent, trying to put himself in her place. What must it be like, he wondered, to be a female with no home, no family, obliged to support oneself? Not, he thought grimly, a desirable situation; yet this girl seemed to have made a go of it. She was a little slip of a thing, too, who looked as though a puff of wind might blow her over; yet there was a firmness about the chin which promised strength of will, and already he knew something of her resourcefulness.

"Tell me about your home," he urged.

"I have no settled home," she replied. "When I was small, my father used to leave me in the care of one of his sisters when he joined his ship. Afterwards, as I grew older, he placed me in a young ladies' seminary in Kensington. He used to come there for me whenever he was ashore and carry me off to some cottage or other on the coast. He could never for long be far from the sight and sound of the sea; he used to say that the nocturnal quiet of an inland village kept him awake at nights—he slept better with the sound of the waves in his ears."

"I suppose he had been at sea since he was a boy?" asked the man.

She nodded. He could see from the expression of her eyes that her thoughts were far away.

"He joined the Navy as a midshipman, and had risen to the rank of Captain when—"

She broke off, and looked away out of the window. The trees and hedges dripped incessantly, mournfully. Great pools, half snow, half water, lay over the fields, and the coach wheels threw up fountains of grey slush which spattered the windows.

After a while, she turned to him again, tilting her chin in a courageous gesture which to the man seemed infinitely pathetic.

"It was the life he loved, and the end he would have chosen," she said. "I should not mourn for him."

The man's eyes softened. Here was a loyal heart, for one who could deserve it.

"He meant a great deal to you."

"He was all I had," she answered simply.

A silence fell between them. He stared out of the window in his turn. It was not far now to London: once there, what would happen to him? Would this lawyer fellow be able to help him? Or was he doomed to wander for ever in a twilight world of ignorance? Impatiently, he pushed these disturbing thoughts away, breaking the silence.

"And after—" he paused, not wishing to refer again to her father's death—"after you left school, where did you make your home?"

"I became a governess. There was insufficient for me to subsist upon—my father was of an optimistic turn of mind, and prize money is variable, you know. I have a little income, but not nearly enough for my needs."

"But have you no relatives who would have made themselves responsible for you?" he asked, indignantly. "You spoke of an aunt—"

"Oh, yes," she replied quietly. "My father's relatives offered—but they are not wealthy people, and I couldn't bring myself to impose upon them."

"And your mother's?"

She hesitated. "We have never had anything to do with my mother's family: indeed, I was never told their name. She—she married to disoblige them, as the saying is, and they never communicated with her afterwards."

He nodded: so the mother had evidently sprung from a family either wealthier or of better social position than the father's.

"But could you not have appealed to them in the circumstances? It would have been possible to find out who they were."

Her head went up.

"I do not appeal for charity, sir."

"To support a female of one's own house is not charity," he protested, "but a simple duty."

"I am persuaded that it is a duty for which my relatives would have had no inclination—nor would I, indeed. Why, they had never even bothered to condole with Papa on his loss, although he informed them of my mother's death. He told me so once, with bitterness that was unusual in him, generous-spirited as he always was!"

He regarded her flushed cheeks, and saw that it was best not to pursue this subject.

"I see. And so for five years you have supported yourself, Miss Spencer. How do you find it, being a governess?"

She gave a little grimace. "Oh, it is well enough. It provides me with a roof over my head and a modest income. But I could sometimes wish that my charges were not quite so high-spirited!"

"They would be," he said grimly. "Spoilt brats, I dare say."

"Well, I must confess—" she began, then broke off, and laughed. "Most likely I was just as bad myself at that age!" she finished.

"I do not think so."

She coloured a little, but spoke lightly. "Do not be deceived by my present manner, sir. No doubt I am much changed since those days."

"I think you are," he said, leaning towards her. "Why do you wear your hair so?"

The abruptness of the question took her by surprise, and for a moment she could say nothing in reply.

"Forgive me," he said, quickly. "I become impertinent again."

"No," she protested. "It is just that—it has been so long since there was anyone to take the kind of interest in me that would prompt such a remark—but you must not think that I resent it. I will try to explain to you how it was."

She leaned back in her corner to steady herself from the jolting of the coach, which was particularly violent at that moment.

"I was not quite eighteen when my father died," she said. "My lawyer brought me the news—the gentleman whom we are to see today. He explained my financial position to me, and it became obvious that I must find some way of improv-

ing it. There seemed only one thing to be done; to obtain a
post as governess or companion in some genteel family."

He nodded. What else was a gentlewoman fitted for? Yet
he felt his indignation rising at the thought of this girl with
the bright hair and soft voice being reduced to such shifts at
a time of life when most young ladies were about to embark
upon a whirl of gaiety.

"I inserted an advertisement in one of the journals," went
on Jane.

"Oh, yes, I've seen such advertisements," he cut in, laughing. "Did you say that it was your delight to improve young
minds? They usually run something on those lines, if my
recollection serves me."

"Not precisely." She smiled at him, revealing small, even
teeth. "I doubt my ability to improve anyone's mind. At any
rate, I had two replies, and arranged an interview with the
writer of the first. This appointment I attended in all the
glory of a new bonnet, with my hair dressed in its accus-
tomed style."

"Ringlets?"

She nodded. "Yes. They were then worn slightly longer
than is the fashionable look today. But I soon discovered my
mistake; of course, I looked by far too young like that. The
lady decided that I would not suit."

"I see," he said, leaning forward and resting his chin in the
palm of his hand as he studied her face. "So you decided to
get rid of your curls?"

"Yes. I found that if I braided my hair like this, I could
add two or three years to my apparent age. I also took care
not to appear too smart at the second interview. I even bor-
rowed cook's second-best bonnet for the occasion!"

He threw back his head in laughter, a gesture that put her
once more in mind of her father. They were not really alike,
of course; strange, though, how the few similarities between
them should fasten on her attention.

"And did you succeed that time?"

"I did. The lady said that she thought I was a trifle young
for the post, but that I had the look of a sensible young
woman: and she thought I ought to be able to manage her
dearest Dorinda, who, although just a little high-spirited, was
of course, the sweetest girl in the world."

"And was she?"

"We-ell." Jane pursed her lips consideringly. "I must say
that the high spirits were more in evidence than the sweet-

ness. But we did well enough together until the time came for her to go to school."

"So that is why your hair is so severely drawn off your face," he said slowly, his glance resting on her small-featured face with a judicial look in his eyes. "I should like to see it—"

He broke off, and was silent. She raised an enquiring eyebrow.

"Nothing," he said hastily, avoiding her eyes.

At that moment, one of the coach wheels found a rut in the road; the vehicle lurched violently, throwing Jane forward from her seat. The man put out his arms to steady her, and for a brief moment she was clasped close to him. His eyes lingered on the soft lips so tantalisingly near to his, on the fine grey eyes, which suddenly held an expression of— what? Confusion?

Suddenly, a wild longing came over him to tighten his hold on her-yielding body, to loosen the warm hair so that it would fall about her face, to press his lips to hers. The strength of his impulse amazed and disconcerted him. With an effort, he choked back the words of endearment that came unbidden to his lips, and placed Jane gently back on the seat, his face tense, his eyes studiously turned from hers.

CHAPTER V

DISCOVERY OF A LETTER

FOR A long time afterwards, they sat in silence, each busy with thoughts that could not be shared. Jane came to herself first, exclaiming because they were about to enter the City. On arriving at London Bridge, they encountered a stream of vehicles; heavy brewers' drays, carts up from the country laden with hay or vegetables, post-chaises and an occasional fashionable town coach.

Every time Jane visited London, she was struck afresh by its bustle and vitality. Now she watched with eager eyes all the varied surging activity around her. The porters were swinging along with baskets atop their heads, mingling with workmen in leather jackets and aprons and grave clerks busy on errands. Each jostled the other good-humouredly in a headlong rush to reach his particular destination in the shortest possible time. Scattered among these hurrying people were the more leisurely pedestrians—the sellers of milk carried in pails attached to a yoke over their shoulders, the vendors of hot rolls with their bells ringing incessantly, the flower women with their gay baskets and cries of "Sweet lavender!" The din made by all these people, added to the thunder of wheels as the vehicles rolled over the cobbled streets and the lowing of a herd of cattle being driven to the markets, was almost deafening. It did not appear to disgust Jane.

"London!" she said, with a sparkle in her eye, "What City is quite like it?"

But her companion did not reply. Like her he was staring from the window, but he seemed sunk in apathy. He continued moody and silent until the stage coach, with a triumphant blast of its horn, drew up at last in the yard of the Crown Inn. He roused himself then sufficiently to see after her baggage, which consisted of a modest carpet bag. She decided to leave this at the Crown to be called for later, and they hailed a passing hackney to convey them the short distance to the offices of Jane's lawyer in Chancery Lane.

They soon arrived; Jane's companion paid off the jarvey, and accompanied her to the door of the building. On the threshold, he hesitated.

"No doubt you will wish to be private with your man of affairs at first," he said. "I will take a turn or two about the street, and perhaps the clerk will summon me when your lawyer shall be ready to receive me."

"Will you not rather wait inside?" asked Jane.

He shook his head.

"No, thank you. I have had more than enough of sitting during the last few hours, and shall be glad of an opportunity of stretching my legs for a while. I will await your pleasure, then."

With a brief bow, he turned to leave her. She watched him run down the steps to the street with a queer little sense of misgiving at her heart. Almost she called after him in an endeavour to persuade him to change his mind; but she had no wish to presume upon what was after all a short, even if an unconventional acquaintance. As she passed through the door, she reflected how strange it was to realise that she had never met this gentleman before last night; today, he seemed so much a part of her life.

The clerk in the outer office informed Jane that Mr. Sharratt would be pleased to see her at once. She followed the man a short distance along a dingy passage smelling of old papers and ink, until they reached a door bearing the lawyer's name. Here the clerk tapped, waiting for an answer before admitting Jane to the presence.

Mr. Sharratt rose from his swivel chair very promptly for one of his years, and welcomed his client with all the cordiality that a naturally precise manner would permit. He was a thin, angular man who stooped a little, with sparse white hair which had receded from a high forehead, and shrewd eyes of a faded blue. He had been the Captain's man of affairs since before Jane's birth, and was intimately acquainted with her history. He now begged her to be seated, placing a comfortable chair for her close to the fire; and proceeded to inquire minutely into matters of her health and affairs in general. As he was almost her only friend nowadays, with the exception of the relatives whom she saw too infrequently for intimacy, she bore patiently with his longwindedness. She was longing to have done with her own concerns, and come to those of the stranger who was waiting below.

She managed at last to mention the original purpose of her visit, which was to release some of her small capital for the purchase of new clothes.

"For you see," she explained, "I cannot very well go as a companion in a nobleman's household with my present wardrobe."

"This will be the first time you have taken a post as a companion, will it not, Miss Jane?"

She nodded, a little uncertainly. "I hope I shall contrive to give satisfaction. Little was said concerning my duties; I only hope that the lady is not too peevish or sickly. I had no means of judging, as I was interviewed by the husband. He was, I should say, in his early fifties, so she cannot be of any great age. I must confess that I should have preferred another post as governess; but none offered, and I cannot afford to wait."

He drew a leather case from his pocket, and fitted a pair of spectacles on to his sharp nose.

"You have not signed any contract, my dear young lady, I trust?"

"Oh, no, Mr. Sharratt. I would not do so without first obtaining your advice."

He nodded, satisfied. "Who is this nobleman?"

"The Earl of Bordesley; his house is in Grosvenor Square."

The dusty blue eyes quickened. The lawyer opened his lips as though about to speak, then shut them again in a firm, thin line, and pondered for several minutes.

"Just so," he said at last. "Well, Miss Jane, I need not tell you that if there is anything you do not like about your new situation, you must come at once to me."

"Why do you say that?" she asked quickly. "Have you any reason to suppose that there will be something I shall not like?"

"Simply a precautionary measure," he told her. "I think you know, my dear, that Mrs. Sharratt and I—but I believe we have spoken of this before."

Jane knew that he referred to an offer, made some years since, to take her into his home as his daughter. The grey eyes warmed and softened.

"I can't accept, sir; impossible for me to tell you how much I value your goodness, your friendship, but I must keep my independence."

He sighed. "We understand; and let me say that we admire the fortitude with which you have met your reverses. However, Miss Jane, beware of too much independence; you, who are always so prompt in coming to the assistance of others, ought to be willing to accept a like service from them. However, I'll not tease you further on that subject at present. How much money will you require?"

Jane named a sum which was the minimum on which she could expect to refurbish her wardrobe suitably for her new post. The lawyer appeared satisfied, and undertook to furnish her with funds at once. He explained that the necessary steps to be taken for the release of her money would take a day or two, but that he was quite at liberty to let her have an advance immediately.

"That is splendid!" said Jane. "And you will not forget to take your fee sir?"

"Naturally," he replied, his face devoid of expression. The plain fact was that he had never yet taken a fee from Miss Spencer, and had no intention of beginning now. It would not do, though, to let her know that.

"When do you take up your new post?"

She frowned. "I stated tomorrow as the time, thinking to give myself two days' grace for my shopping; but I was delayed upon the road, and now shall have only one. That reminds me, sir, there is something—"

"You will sleep with us tonight, I trust?" he cut in quickly. "I will send a note to Mrs. Sharratt; there is always a room ready for you, as you know."

Jane thanked him, and, before he could turn the conversation, hurried on to tell him the story of her strange adventure on the road. He listened with some misgivings; it was infamous that such a dear, sweet girl should be subjected to dangers of the kind. Mrs. Sharratt and he had no children of their own, and they would have taken her into their household and thanked Heaven for the privilege. But it was no use; she had all her father's courage and resolution, and a pride which perhaps came from the mother's side. His face was grave when she had finished her tale.

"You must be a little more upon your guard, my dear; this man may be anyone. Indeed, the whole business might be a trick to trap the unwary."

"What, to have oneself knocked on the head outside a modest inn?" asked Jane, with a trace of indignation in her tone.

"No, not that, of course, but his statement that he had lost his memory might well be false. You do not know what crimes he may have to cover."

"I would stake my life on his integrity!" declared Jane, emphatically.

Dismay crossed the lawyer's face. The girl seemed by far too taken up with this unknown man. He knew women well enough, however, to judge that any opposition on his part would serve only to heighten the interest, and therefore he held his peace. He rang for the clerk, desiring him to fetch up the gentleman whom he would find waiting outside.

"What name, sir?" asked the clerk.

"No name," was the brief answer.

The clerk gaped.

"Well, do you mean to go? I dare say you won't encounter a dozen or so of gentlemen lingering in the vicinity," remarked Mr. Sharratt, with an irritability usual in him when he was worried.

"You cannot mistake him," put in Jane, eagerly. "He is tall and dark, with thick black eyebrows and a penetrating sort of look."

"At once, ma'am," said the clerk, hurrying from the room.

Mr. Sharratt scowled a little over Jane's description, which to his mind conveyed the picture of a very villain. They sat in silence for what seemed a long time, before footsteps were heard in the passage outside. Jane sprang to her feet, hastily pushing back her chair, so that it nearly overturned.

The door opened, revealing the bemused and slightly sheepish face of the clerk.

"Beg pardon, sir, but there's no gentleman outside."

"Nonsense!" cried Jane, almost sharply. Once again her heart contracted with misgiving. "He must be there—did you look farther along the street?"

"Yes, ma'am," replied the man, timidly. "I walked up and down a bit, but I encountered no one but a neighbour of ours."

"I must see for myself," said Jane, and ran impetuously from the room before Mr. Sharratt could stop her.

Her feet scarcely seemed to touch the ground as she sped along the passage, through the front office, and down the steps into the street. Here she halted, and looked about her.

He must be here. How long had she been talking with the lawyer? Perhaps twenty minutes, even a half-hour: he might have gone quite a distance in that time, strolling about, preoccupied with his thoughts. He would most likely return presently, dismayed to find that he had been so long absent. But at any rate, the clerk was right; the gentleman was not here now.

Inexplicably, she suddenly knew that he was gone and would not return. She had known it from the moment when they had parted outside the building, the moment when she had wanted to call him back.

With feet that dragged, she made the journey back to Mr. Sharratt's room. He looked up expectantly as she entered, frowning at seeing her alone.

"Sit down, my dear," he said gently.

His client looked as if she had suffered a shock.

Jane seated herself in a dazed fashion, and remained silent for some minutes.

"Where can he be?" she burst out at last. "I must confess I feel anxious about his welfare—how will he fare alone in his present condition?"

The lawyer cleared his throat. "Assuming that the story he told you was true—"

Jane's eyes flashed. "I thought we had disposed of that quibble!"

"Just so," said Mr. Sharratt, soothingly. "There remain, then, as I see it, two possibilities. Either he has gone on some errand, and will presently be back—"

Jane shook her head despondently. "I thought of that; but we have been sitting here an age. He has had time to return from any little call at a shop, and what other errand could he have?"

The lawyer nodded. "I do not depend too much upon my first supposition. My second is that he has recovered his memory while we have been talking here, and set off immediately for his home, wherever that may be."

Jane turned this over in her mind. It seemed reasonable enough, and yet—. "But do you think that—that he would go without first telling me? After all that we have shared—" she broke off, blushing.

"At first sight, it may appear as an ungrateful action," replied the lawyer. "But examine it closely, and you will decide that it is only a natural one. The man suddenly remembers who he is and where he lives, and his first thought is to reach home without delay. Later, no doubt, he will seek you out and thank you for your assistance."

"I want no thanks!" said Jane quickly. "It was not that, but—well, I had come to think of him as a friend."

The lawyer gave her a shrewd glance, but held his tongue.

"I was going to help him discover his identity," continued Jane. "In a way, it was exciting—a kind of adventure; and now it has ended so tamely!"

Mr. Sharratt nodded sympathetically. His own thought was that this fellow had taken himself off in the nick of time. The odds were that he was some undesirable or other, and, had he stayed, complications must have ensued. Evidently there was no point in putting his thoughts into words, however. His client was a woman, therefore impressionable. Too marked an opposition on his part could serve only to strengthen the fancy which had seized her for this unknown man; it must be left to time to eradicate the unfortunate impression.

"There is the snuff box!" exclaimed Jane, suddenly. "What should I do about that, sir?"

"May I see it?" he asked.

She opened her reticule, and placed the box on the table. He picked it up, and examined it minutely. It was a square box of gold, rather deep, and ornamented with an enamelled likeness of a grape-vine, set in rubies and emeralds. On the underside of the box was a single cluster of grapes. Mr. Sharratt flicked open the lid, but shook his head in disappointment.

"There's nothing here to guide us to the owner."

"I know. He had the same idea himself," Jane replied.

The lawyer closed the lid again, and revolved the box thoughtfully in his hands.

"It is rather deeper than most trinkets of the kind," he said, musingly. "I do believe—"

He broke off, and examined once more the base of the box.

"Look, Miss Jane, here is a groove! The bottom of the box slides off!"

He suited the action to the word, placing the thin gold lid on the table and revealing a small compartment in the base of the snuff box. In it rested a single sheet of flimsy folded paper.

He looked hesitantly at Jane. "I feel that, in the circumstances, perhaps—"

"Yes, yes!" she cried, impatiently. "You must open it, of course! It may lead us to the owner!"

Her face was flushed with excitement. He took the paper

out, unfolded it, and read. Jane peered eagerly over his shoulder as he did so.

There was no address at the head of the paper, which was written in an obviously feminine hand.

"Beloved" it began:

"I can wait no longer to throw myself into your arms. F. is to be absent from home tonight and tomorrow. If you will come to me after midnight, my maid will be waiting, as I shall, my own life. C."

A long silence fell in the room. Jane remained motionless, her head bowed over the paper, her hands tightly clenched together in her lap. Mr. Sharratt glanced quickly at her, then turned his attention once more to the letter. He cleared his throat uneasily.

"H'm. It seems we have stumbled upon a private matter which does not, in any case, lead us to our objective. There is no saying who the lady is, but it sounds very much as though F would prove to be a deceived husband. However, we need not concern ourselves with a document we ought never to have seen in the first place. If I might venture to advise you in this, Miss Jane, I think it would be as well to banish all thoughts of this unknown man. He may return to render his thanks to you for your service, and to reclaim his property. Perhaps you would like me to take charge of it for you, and then you can simply refer him to me."

She raised her eyes, and he saw the pain in them.

"Yes," she replied, in a low tone. "Yes, perhaps that would be best."

Her eyes strayed back to the letter. He took it up quickly and replaced it in the box, a grim expression round his mouth. It was a thousand pities that this girl, of all women, should have run across such a scoundrel. Here, he knew, was a loyal, affectionate heart; and, since her father's death, there had been no one on whom she could fix it. Such a girl, lonely, homeless, friendly and loving, was fair prey for every unscrupulous monster who crossed her path: so thought Mr. Sharratt.

Jane's thoughts were of quite another kind; indeed, she was so confused that she could not then have analysed them. She watched dumbly while the lawyer went to a safe and locked away the snuff box; and when he returned to the table, placing some banknotes before her, she had not moved.

"There was a matter of some new clothes, was there not?" he asked, in an endeavour to rouse her from her abstraction.

She started as though rudely awakened from a deep sleep.

"Yes, yes, of course," she said. There was a pause: then, speaking with more animation in her voice—"What time do you desire my return here, sir?"

"My time is at your disposal," replied the lawyer. "How long do such commissions generally take?"

Jane consulted the clock which stood over the fireplace. It showed half past one.

"I will be here again before five o'clock," she promised.

Her manner was now almost as it had been during their earlier conversation. Mr. Sharratt nodded approvingly. She could not know that his approval was for her self-control.

CHAPTER VI

MY LADY BORDESLEY

AT A LITTLE after ten o'clock on the following morning, my Lady Bordesley was alone in her boudoir. The handsome apartment was furnished in a style calculated to induce tranquillity, from the soft tones of the pink puckered satin wallpaper to the thick carpet which muffled all harsh sound: yet my lady fidgeted from one seat to another, now choosing the striped silk sofa, now perching on a stool reluctantly embroidered by her own hand to while away the tedium of evenings spent in Bordesley's company. Even when seated, she could not be still; for her small foot in its pink satin slipper tapped restlessly, and her white hand plucked nervously at the ribands and lace adorning her peignoir.

She was a beautiful creature, fashionably dark, with blue-glinting curls which clung softly to a white neck, and an oval face of perfect features. At one time, her charms had been renowned in that kind of verse which it pleased the gentlemen of fashion to write; for, until her marriage to Bordesley, she had been one of the Toasts of the Town. Her large, innocent-seeming blue eyes had then been the cause of many a broken friendship, and even of duels. In vain, however; after many inconsistencies of affection, the Incomparable Celia had finally given her hand into the safe keeping of a nobleman thirty years her senior.

My Lord Bordesley was a man who knew how to guard his own. In a short space, his jealousy had driven to a discreet distance even the most daring of the young bucks who had previously formed his wife's court. This, perhaps, came as a surprise to that young woman herself. When she had wed my lord, she had not for one moment imagined that matrimony would seriously interfere with her diversions. The façade which Bordesley showed to the world was one of cultured indolence, and she had believed herself capable of twisting him around her little finger—a favorite occupation

41

of hers with the opposite sex. Time had shown her the error of this belief: behind my lord's mask lay a strength of feeling hitherto unsuspected.

Being above all things a practical young woman, for some time after her marriage, she had been content to cut her gown according to her cloth. She had decided, with a shrug, that the loss of her following was one of the prices to be paid for the acquiring of a title and fortune. But a year or so of being the object of only one man's attentions was more than enough for her: and rumour had it that, for some while now, my lady Bordesley had been amusing herself at her lord's expense.

This morning the beauty of her face was somewhat marred by a petulant expression, and her blue eyes reflected the uneasiness that plagued her mind. When could she expect to hear—today? Just possibly today, she mused, but far more likely tomorrow. Tomorrow! It was a thousand ages until then! Another sleepless night loomed before her. Why, oh, why had she ever been such a fool in the first place as to put herself in his power? Her mind conjured up the image of his careless laughing eyes, and mocking smile. He was possessed of something of the quality that she herself had, she acknowledged grudgingly: it was difficult to be level-headed where he was concerned.

Her thoughts turned briefly to the other man. She smiled contemptuously. Poor Richard! She remembered his white set face when he had confronted her with the notice of her engagement in the Gazette, four years since. He seemed to have believed then that he was the one she had intended to marry. She had carried that interview off well, she told herself complacently, managing at one and the same time to convince the young man of her firmness of purpose to wed Bordesley, and of her undying, though purely sisterly, affection for himself. She had brought him to see that any other notions he might have been harbouring were quite mistaken. He had quitted her resigned to his fate, believing she had chosen the better man. He seemed more deeply in love than ever, and had sworn that, if ever he could serve her, he would come from the ends of the earth to do so.

Highly satisfactory, thought my lady; and yet ... There had been a difference in him two nights ago, when he had stood here in the boudoir beside her. Until that moment, they had not met for four years, except briefly in full company at some fashionable gathering or other. The impetuous, idealistic boy had vanished; in his place was a man, sardonic, cynical even. Yet she knew that her influence over him was not quite lost; there had been a moment, when she had dropped her handkerchief, and their hands had touched . . . She smiled to herself like a cat that has got at the cream.

With a swirl of her soft draperies, she moved gracefully to the bell-rope. An abigail entered the room.

"You rang, m'lady?"

"Yes, Betty. Find me the Lady's Magazine. I left it—I know not where, but find it. And quickly, mistress! None of your dawdling, or I'll make your ears sing for you!"

The girl bobbed, and lowered her eyes to hide the hate that flooded them. If the fates had so willed it, she, Betty, might now have been calling the tune for my fine lady to dance. Well, that fool Perkins had bungled things, thrown away the chance of a lifetime, and lost a good job into the bargain. Now there was little likelihood of their being able to marry, and of her escaping from the slavery of my lady's service.

She hurried from the room, mindful of the lady's threat. As her hand turned the doorknob, her eye fell upon the shrivelled skin of the burn across her fingers. That had been caused last week by my lady pettishly thrusting aside the curling irons. There was many a score to be paid off in that quarter, she thought viciously as she hurriedly searched the drawing room for the book. Thanks to Perkins, this time she had missed her opportunity of achieving this end; but one day, she promised herself, the debt should be paid in full.

The Lady's Magazine was found behind the curtains in one of the window-seats. Betty hurried with it to her mistress, fearful of being punished for having been too long about her task; but my lady said nothing, merely snatching the book, and dismissing the abigail.

The mistress seated herself on the sofa, riffling idly through the pages of the book. Anything was better than having one's mind going round in circles. She turned to the new season's fashions. Classic simplicity was the prevailing note of the present mode, with skirts falling in soft folds from a waistline situated just under the bosom. Simplicity did not appeal overmuch to Lady Bordesley: still, one had to be in the fashion. Perhaps such a gown as this might not look so very demure if one damped it slightly to make it cling to the figure, as was the custom in France? Yes, that might answer. This particular gown, now, in green or lavender, should be most becoming to her with her white skin and glossy dark hair.

But no, she was forgetting! She must still wear the drab colours of mourning, for Francis was a stickler for the conventions, and his father not yet six weeks dead. It was absurd, for what had she cared for the grim, bitter old man whose death had elevated her to the rank of Countess? In her opinion, this was the only thing of interest that he had ever done. She decided that she would be hanged if she would wear black any more; she meant to tell Francis so, though not perhaps just in that downright way. That would not answer with Bordesley. There were ways, however, of cajoling him.

Suddenly it came to her that life was inexpressibly tedious: always so much scheming to get one's own way. With an exasperated exclamation, she flung the magazine from her across the room.

It took the Earl squarely between the eyes as he entered. He betrayed no sign of surprise beyond a lifted eyebrow, and coolly stooped to retrieve the book, tossing it on to a low table.

"A fit of the sullens, my life?"

There was something in his tone that made her uneasy. She could handle Francis when he was madly in love or jealous, for drama was the element in which she moved most gracefully. Sarcasm or amusement put her sadly out of step, however. She set herself to charm him into a more propitious mood.

"I am so happy now that you are come!" she exclaimed, running towards him and throwing her arms around his neck in a pretty gesture. "Did I hurt your poor head?"

She rubbed the spot where the book had landed with a soft hand, murmuring endearments the while. The Earl's expression changed, and for a time it looked as though Celia's intention of charming him had succeeded too well for her purpose. She was skillful enough at steering through these deep waters, however, and presently judged that she might safely broach the subject on her mind.

"Francis, you do like to see me looking pretty, do you not?"

He assented, attempting to draw her close again.

"No, no, you are naughty! But, Francis, how can I look my best in this hideous black? There are some quite delightful gowns in the Lady's Magazine, and it is too depressing to think that I may not order any of them in a more becoming shade!"

He frowned. "It is barely six weeks since my father's death," he reminded her.

Celia pouted. "Oh, yes, I know, but what purpose can be served by my going in dark colours for ever? I long for something bright, something gay—coquelicot ribands, emerald green silk—even white muslin would be preferable to this eternal black!"

"A pretty shade of grey, perhaps?" suggested the Earl. "Anything else would cause comment, I imagine."

"Oh, fustian! If one is to take account of gossiping, one would do nothing! I may not go to balls and assemblies while we are in mourning; that is hardship enough, surely! It makes life insupportably dull!"

The Earl regarded her thoughtfully for a moment, then seated himself on the sofa, placing his finger tips together with a judicial air.

"That aspect of the situation had occurred to me already, Celia. I would not wish you to lack company at this—or, indeed, at any other time; and so I hit upon a plan."

Celia gave him a suspicious look.

"A plan?"

"I do make them sometimes, my fairest life," replied her husband, drily. "I am aware that you consider me to be the most indolent of fellows—not, I fear, without cause; but in this instance, you will be obliged to allow me credit for some exertion. I propose to enliven the tedium of your remaining months of mourning—" he paused, and regarded his finger nails with interest "—with the society of a hired companion."

"You—?"

It could never be said that my lady Bordesley ever did anything so unfeminine as to gasp; nevertheless, she came very close to it now. She collapsed on to the nearest chair, and stared at her husband incredulously. He put up one hand to smooth his greying, once auburn, hair, and returned her look equably.

"A companion, my love. Someone to bear you company during your hours of enforced segregation from the crowds of which you are so enamoured."

There was a faint tinge of bitterness in his tone. Celia let it pass, too taken up with the content of his speech.

"A companion!" she repeated, in horror. "A dreary, dowdy, elderly female to hang around me with an everlasting piece of embroidery, driving me slowly mad! Oh, no, no, no!"

She jumped up, stamping her foot. It only added to her ir-
ritation to find that the thickness of the carpet rendered this
gesture ineffective.

The Earl smiled maddeningly.

"Dowdy, perhaps," he said, consideringly. "Dreary, elderly,
addicted solely to needlework—no, I don't think so."

"You sound as though you had already fixed upon someone," said Celia, in alarm.

"Yes, my dear, I have. I interviewed a young woman for
the post at Rochester, some weeks back. She satisfied my re-
quirements, but was unable to come here immediately. I received a note from her by this morning's post, however, and
she is to present herself here at eleven o'clock. I feel sure you
will find her agreeable company."

"Well!"

Amazement and indignation wrestled for control of Celia's
countenance. It was some time before she could say more.

"May I know," she managed at last acidly, "why a step
which concerns me so nearly was taken without my knowledge or consent?"

"It is as I told you, my love," replied the Earl, gently. "I
would not wish you to be lonely."

"That is rubbish, Francis, and you know it! I may still see
my friends, and attend small private parties, and so I do!
Why, only tomorrow I am bid to join Selina and her sister at
the play, and the day after that I am to go to a musical
party! I need never be alone, as you well know!"

The Earl once more regarded his finger nails. A fire had
crept into his green eyes.

"I find I do not care for your friends, Celia."

"And so you mean to foist this female upon me! I thank
you! Well, you've only yourself to blame if she finds that, after all, she is not suited for the post!"

The Earl raised his eyes to her heated countenance; they
held a distinct menace. In many ways, Celia could bend him
to her will, but there was a point beyond which she dared not
go.

"She will remain," he stated calmly, "for some months, at
any rate. You may as well make up your mind to that, my
dear."

Celia saw that she must capitulate for the moment, but did
not despair. On another occasion, Francis might be in a more
pliant mood, and the companion would vanish as quickly as

she had come. Managing the Earl of Bordesley was entirely a matter of choosing one's moment.

"Oh, very well!" she said, with only a slight show of petulance. "What kind of female is she?"

The Earl considered before answering.

"She struck me as being a sensible, intelligent young woman, but that does not altogether convey her personality."

He hesitated again.

"There was a warmth about her that is difficult to define," he continued at last. "One felt that she might be someone to turn to in time of trouble. Also, I had the impression that she was possessed of a distinct sense of humour, though held discreetly in check."

"She sounds tedious," pronounced his wife. She eyed her husband shrewdly. Was it possible that he had his own reasons for introducing this woman into his household? She had thought that she had guessed his aim; namely, to add one more to the spies that surrounded her. There had been that in his manner and tone, however, that suggested a personal interest.

Almost she frowned, but checked herself in time; frowning had an ageing effect, and, moreover, it would be bad policy to allow Francis to see that she suspected anything other than appeared on the surface.

She must be losing her hold over him, though, if he was looking around for amours. Perhaps she had been a shade too petulant, too demanding, of late; that must be cured. He was at the dangerous age: let him once take a fancy to another woman, and Celia's days as a Countess were numbered. It would not be difficult for him to find proof enough to divorce her. All that now prevented him from doing so was the fact that he still lay under her spell. He might spy on her, and makes jealous scenes, but she knew well that he did not really want to find conclusive proof of her infidelity. If it were presented to him, though, irrefutable proof—she turned hot and cold as she thought of the matter that had been in the forefront of her mind for the past week or more. With an effort that left no trace on the beautiful face, she mastered her thoughts.

"How old is this paragon?" she asked.

"About your age, I should say."

"My age!" Celia's alarm increased. "A companion of my age?"

"One supposes they must begin some time," replied the Earl, amused.

"I hope she is a gentlewoman," remarked Celia acidly, forgetting her good intentions.

"I did not question her concerning her ancestry. She had some excellent references from unexceptionable sources, and was obviously of good birth. I flatter myself, perhaps unduly in your opinion, that I am no mean judge of people."

Celia had to admit this. Francis was remarkably shrewd in his dealings with everyone except herself.

"But you admitted yourself that she is a dowd," she objected, in a milder tone. "How, then, do you expect me to take her amongst my friends—for I collect that you do?"

"Do you suppose," countered the Earl, "that a smart, attractive governess would be welcome in most households? It seemed to me that this young woman had determined to guard against rejection on those grounds. Also, perhaps, a lack of means—"

Here he was interrupted by a knock upon the door. A servant entered and announced that a Miss Spencer was asking for his lordship.

"Show her up," commanded the Earl.

Turning to his wife, he said, "Now, my dear, you will have an opportunity of judging for yourself."

Celia turned her eyes impatiently towards the door. She was curious to see the woman who could inspire so much confidence in anyone as shrewd as my lord.

After an interval, the servant knocked once more. The door opened to admit a young woman, who greeted them in a soft, musical voice. She was becomingly, though not expensively, dressed in what appeared to be a new grey pelisse trimmed with yellow corded ribbon. Her bonnet was tied under her chin with strings of the same yellow. The colour brought out the hidden lights in the chestnut curls which framed her face.

Recognition was instant.

"Celia Walbrook!"

"By all that's wonderful—Jane Tarrant!"

The exclamation was simultaneous: each started forward a step, oblivious of the Earl, who appeared equally surprised.

Celia, ever quick-witted, was the first to recover herself.

"Upon my word, this is extraordinary! Who could have supposed, my lord, that you would bring me an old schoolfellow as companion?"

Then, turning to Jane, who stood uncertainly by the door, looking more than a little dismayed; "But you have my name wrong. I am no longer Celia Walbrook, but Celia Bordesley. It seems that you, too, are no longer Jane Tarrant. Are you, then, married?"

CHAPTER VII

ENCOUNTER AT THE PLAY

"Pray be seated, Miss-er-Spencer," said the Earl, smoothly, indicating a chair.

Jane sank gratefully into it, her colour a little heightened.

"So you and my wife were at school together. Dear me, how very odd a coincidence!"

Jane agreed, somewhat breathlessly, thinking that it was a most uncomfortable coincidence. If she had known that my lady Bordesley was the erstwhile Celia Walbrook, nothing would have induced her to set foot in the Bordesley household. Young people at school together do not take long to learn the truth about each other, and nothing that Jane remembered of the girl Celia gave her any encouragement to hope for an amicable relationship with my lady Bordesley.

Celia saw her discomforture, and pressed home her advantage.

"Then you cannot be married, Jane, for my husband calls you Miss Spencer. Do, pray, tell me what the mystery is!"

She had the satisfaction of seeing Jane's embarrassment deepen.

"There is no mystery, my lady," she replied, after a pause to collect herself. "After my father's death, I found myself obliged to earn a living. I was christened Jane Spencer Tarrant: I decided it might be better to use only my first two names."

"How discreet of you!" said Celia, sweetly. "But then you were always the soul of discretion, as I remember. I believe no one ever heard where you went when you left Miss Leasowe's establishment, not even your nearest and dearest friends."

Jane's eyes flashed at the insulting tone of the remark. It was true that she had dropped all her friends when her circumstances changed, not wishing to be an embarrassment to

51

them. It was for the same reason that she had changed her name.

"We all thought it most odd," went on Celia, enjoying herself. "There were a good many rumours, as I remember. Some had it that you had made a runaway match; while others thought that you had gone to live with impoverished relatives, and were too ashamed to introduce them to our acquaintance."

She did not think it worthwhile to add that she herself had started these rumours; but Jane's previous knowledge of Celia enabled her to guess this. The colour flamed in her face.

"I see now that we were not so far out in our surmises," finished my lady, with a malicious smile. "Indeed, it is a pity that you should have so much come down in the world, Jane—and Miss Leasowe's seminary was so select, too!"

"I think that Miss Spencer may desire to be shown her room," interposed the Earl at this point. He had no taste for watching Celia play cat and mouse.

He rose and went to the bell-rope. A servant appeared, and Jane took her leave with a hot cheek and a grateful glance at his lordship.

"A very pretty exhibition of feminine behaviour, my dear," he said drily to Celia.

"I owe her a few knocks!" exclaimed his wife, with a hard look in the blue eyes.

He raised his brows.

"I dare say you don't know what it is to have someone held up to you as a paragon!"

"When I was at school, we had a short way of dealing with toadies," replied his lordship, reflectively.

"Yes, perhaps, but the thing was, she was popular with the other girls: she might well be, for she used to help half of them with their tasks. She was one of those poor fools who cannot help involving themselves in other people's scrapes!"

"I feel sure that is an error into which you would not be likely to fall," said the Earl, drily.

Celia raised her brows. "Would you applaud me if I did? Bah, it is the worst kind of folly! If I am to be in a scrape, let it be one of my own contriving."

"By all means," he replied. "You contrive them so well."

This was Francis at his most difficult. She went swiftly to his side, twining her soft white arms about his neck. Her voice took on a coaxing tone.

"Why do we talk of Jane Tarrant? I will not oppose you if

you are set on keeping her here. Dearest Francis, let us speak of something else."

He looked deep into her eyes, those blue, unfathomable eyes that had been used to enslave so many men. He touched the soft skin of her neck lightly; her lips curved and invited. He forgot about Miss Spencer.

That young lady had been shown into a room next to Celia's boudoir, a room daintily furnished, and with a fire in the grate, for these last days of March were chilly. At any other time, she would have been full of appreciation, for the apartment was in a more luxurious style than those usually offered to her in her capacity as governess: but just at present, she felt that the meanest hovel would be preferable to sharing a mansion with Celia Bordesley. She would not stay here. Nothing should persuade her to do so!

What, then, would she do, she asked herself? Go to Mr. and Mrs. Sharratt or one of her aunts, until she could find another post? She could not bring herself to be a burden upon any of these good souls, ignoring the fact that they would never have thought of such a word in connection with her visit. What remained? Only to find some modest lodging, and do her utmost to procure another post. And that, she reflected sadly, she could not risk; for her slender means would not allow of protracted idleness, and she might wait many months before a vacancy offered.

Her chin went up resolutely. No, she would stay; she was not going to haul down her colours without showing fight. Before this, she had faced covert sneers and insults without flinching; she had developed a protective armour which had stood her in good stead. Why, then, had it been so easily pierced today? She knew the answer. It was because of the blow she had suffered yesterday. Well, there was no profit in thinking of that affair. It was best to forget, as Mr. Sharratt had counselled.

Surprisingly enough, she found Celia not unfriendly when next they met. True, she seemed to derive a certain pleasure in issuing Jane with orders, but such duties as the latter had appeared to be light. A ribbon that required matching at one of the shops, a stitch dropped in a piece of needlework, a book to be changed at the Circulating Library—such trivial tasks occupied her time for the next two days. Jane began to wonder what need my lady had of a companion, for she certainly did not lack for company. There were morning callers in plenty, and a chattering female who took tea on the first afternoon.

She was somewhat startled at being bidden to attend Celia to the play in the evening of the second day. She could not know that it was by the Earl's expressed wish; and hoped fervently that the simple yellow muslin which she had bought to serve her for evenings, might not compare too unfavourably with the gowns of Celia and her elegant companions.

If Jane had been stirred at the sight of London by day, she found the Town even more fascinating by night. Dozens of smart equipages bowled along over the cobbled streets, passing great houses ablaze with light ready to receive guests, with gold-laced footmen lining the steps. Link-boys with their flaring torches and chairmen bearing elegantly dressed ladies and gentlemen crowded the streets. An impression of glittering festivity remained with her long after she had taken her seat with the rest of Celia's party in the box at the theatre, and the curtain had risen.

Jane had been privileged to watch an occasional private theatrical performance in the houses where she had been employed, but it had not before come in her way to visit the theatre. She was a little put out, therefore, at not being allowed on this occasion to concentrate upon what was going forward on the stage. Celia's friends Lord and Lady Brettle kept up a constant low murmur of conversation; while Celia herself and her bosom friend Selina Breakwell had not even the good manners to keep their tones subdued. More than once, Celia's musical laugh rang out during one of the more impressive speeches, and Jane felt she would dearly liked to box her ears. It puzzled her to know why anyone should bother to visit the theatre, unless with the intention of hearing the play.

During the interval, all five walked up and down outside the box, in common with other members of the audience. Among these, Jane particularly noticed a tall handsome man with fair hair brushed in a seemingly careless style, and amused blue eyes. He checked when he came opposite to Celia's party, and bowed. Celia's companions returned the civility, but Jane noticed that Celia herself wore a cold, distant look on her face. The gentleman appeared to notice this too, for the amusement in his eyes deepened, and he stepped deliberately in front of Celia, thus forcing her to stop in her pacing.

"My lady Bordesley! 'Pon rep, this is a very pleasant encounter! What think you of the play?" Jane heard him say, before Lady Breakwell took her arm and urged her onwards. Lord and Lady Brettle also continued walking, leaving Celia alone to converse with her new-found companion.

She waited until the others were out of earshot, then turned on him in disdain.

"I wonder you have the effrontery to address me!"

He raised one eyebrow, a trick of his which gave him a slightly diabolical air.

"What, Celia? Sulking? Come now, play and pay is the rule, my heart's life!"

"How dare you!" she said, in a low, fierce tone, clenching her small fists. "Leave me this instant, sir!"

"When you are so adorably in looks? Never! It is asking too much of human nature! Besides, why do you wish me to leave you?"

"You may well ask," she replied, in a somewhat milder manner. Try as she might, she could never quite resist his impudence. "Do you think you have behaved in a gentlemanlike way towards me?"

"No," he said softly, leaning nearer to speak in her ear. "Let us say rather in a loverlike way, fairest Celia."

"Do you call it the action of a lover to extort money from me?" she whispered back, furiously.

"But I could not persuade you to make me a gift, my heart's angel; I did beg you to do so, but I found you adamant. What could I then do but turn to barter, and offer to sell you the only thing I possessed which might possibly be of interest to you?"

"I am not made of money," said Celia, with an angry frown. "I have given you quite enough in the past. It was time to call a halt, unless Bordesley were to become suspicious."

"My soul's delight, I have been embarrassing you!" he cried in a contrite tone. "Why did you not tell me so before? I would have found some other means of settling my affairs."

"Tell you before—!" Celia broke off, aghast, then burst out laughing. " 'Pon rep, Julian, your impudence passes all bounds!"

A slow smile spread over his countenance as he watched her anger fading. Even with Celia, his charm never failed to produce the desired effect.

"But what are you doing in Town?" she stopped laughing to ask. "I understood your pockets were to let, and therefore you were obliged to remain in Kent. If I had known, I need scarce have gone to so much trouble—this alters all my plans!"

"I am flattered to think I have the power to alter your plans. I am able to be once more in Town because of your—er—generosity."

"My—?" Celia stared. "But then—" realising the full implication of his statement—"where is my letter?"

He paused in the act of taking a pinch of snuff, and looked keenly at her.

"Have you not received it?"

She shook her head. "What can it mean? You saw Richard, I imagine?"

His face took on the satanic look.

"Yes, I saw him." He shut the snuff box with a snap, returning it to his pocket. "Has he not waited on you, then, to hand you the letter?"

"No, Julian, he has not. What do you suppose it can mean? Of course, there is Francis—but then, Richard might have contrived to send me a message to let me know that all was well. When was he with you?"

"Let me see," he said, carelessly. "Five—no, four days since; very likely he has forgot. You will hear from him soon."

"Four days!" echoed Celia, alarmed. "He would never allow all that time to elapse before sending me word—I know Richard too well! Something must be wrong!"

"You may not know him as well as you think," he said, sardonically. "Perhaps the noble Richard means to turn the document to his own account."

"But no, Julian! He is not in need of money!"

"One may barter with a woman for other things than money," he said, significantly.

She shook her head. "Not Richard," she said, decidedly. "He could not be such a—a blackguard."

He bowed ironically.

She caught his eye, and laughed.

"Oh, well, you are a law unto yourself, Julian! You believe that the end justifies the means, and although you are a thorough rogue, somehow I cannot for long be angry with you!"

"We are two of a kind, my lady," he said, taking her hand and pressing his lips to it; for by this time, the passage was deserted, the interval having ended some minutes since.

She looked up into the mocking eyes, and thrilled to the challenge she found there.

"I almost believe we are," she answered.

They stood thus for a moment, silently sharing a long regard. A low, drawling voice broke suddenly in upon them.

"Good evening, Celia; your servant, Summers. It appears to have escaped your notice that the play has recommenced."

It was the Earl of Bordesley.

CHAPTER VIII

ERRAND TO BROOK STREET

ALONE IN her bedchamber, Jane sat on a low stool before the fire, thinking over the events of the evening. A different atmosphere had fallen over the party in the box when the Earl of Bordesley had joined them after the interval. Jane had been allowed to watch the remainder of the play in peace, for no one showed the least inclination to chatter. There had been something in the Earl's manner, too, a suggestion of menace; could it be, wondered Jane, that he disapproved of his wife's tête-à-tête with the handsome gentleman she had encountered in the passage?

Jane reflected uneasily that perhaps she ought to have remained at Celia's side; but it had been difficult to ignore Lady Breakwell's insistent pressure on her arm without positive incivility. It would seem that my lady Bordesley had no more discretion than the flighty young Celia Walbrook had possessed: a chat with the gentleman would have been perfectly proper had it not been prolonged beyond the moment when everyone else had returned to the play. Jane had seen little of the Earl, but she fancied that such tactics would not answer with him. He would, she felt sure, be jealous of his wife's good name. How foolish in Celia to risk the displeasure of the man she loved for the empty admiration of others! But, of course, it must be difficult for one so bewitchingly lovely to resist the temptation of bringing men to her feet. If Jane's aesthetic sense could appreciate Celia's beauty, it was evident that her appeal to the opposite sex must be strong indeed.

Harsh sounds intruded rudely upon these thoughts. Jane raised her head and listened. Sharp voices came to her ears from Celia's boudoir next door; she could not distinguish the words, but she recognised the Earl's deep tones and Celia's from Celia's boudoir next door; she could not distinguish the found herself involuntarily straining to catch the words, and

59

picked up a book from the table at the side of her bed. She moved the candle-stand nearer to her elbow, and tried to concentrate upon the text.

In a little while, the uproar ceased. She heard Celia's door open, and the Earl's firm footsteps departing down the passage. There was a short interval, and the door opened again: this time, it was evidently Celia's maid who presented herself, for Jane recognised her voice. A sharp sound, as of a slap, quickly followed, and the girl was heard to retreat. Celia's door slammed with finality, and through the dividing wall came the muffled sound of sobbing.

Jane stirred uneasily in her seat. It was against her nature to allow anyone to be miserable without offering such comfort as she was able; but would Celia welcome an intrusion on her grief? She rose as if to go next door, then hesitated, listening. For perhaps five minutes she stood there, immobile, hearing through the wall Celia's unabated sobbing. At last, she could bear it no longer. She left her room quietly, and tapped gently on the door of the boudoir.

There was silence for a moment.

"Who is it?" shouted a muffled voice at last. "Go away!"

The sobs were renewed even more violently than before. Jane opened the door, and edged a trifle into the room.

"It is I, Jane," she began hesitantly. "Celia, what is the matter? Is there anything I can do?"

The other looked up, her lovely face distorted with rage.

"I suppose you have come to crow over me, is that it?" she shouted, wiping the tears away from her cheeks fiercely.

"No such thing, as you very well know," replied Jane calmly. "However, since you have no need of me, I'll say goodnight."

She started to retreat, but Celia ran forward, and, seizing her by the arm, dragged her into the room.

"No, don't go away, Jane. I must talk to someone. Come and sit over here."

She seated herself on the sofa, pulling Jane down beside her.

"I must look a sight," she said ruefully, picking up a glass from a small table nearby, and earnestly contemplating her reflection. She dabbed at her eyes once more, and patted her curls into place.

"It is all Francis's fault! He does put me in such a passion!"

"He seems very kind," said Jane.

"Kind! My dear Jane, you can have no idea! He seems to think that, because I am married to him, I must behave as though I were some heathen female in a seraglio or some such: if he could have me guarded by fierce natives with knives, I am persuaded that he would do so!"

Jane disregarded this poetic flight. "You mean that he is consistently jealous?"

"Jealous! There was never anything like it, I assure you! If I so much as to speak to another man, he has a fit of the sullens!"

"Then perhaps it was not very wise of you to allow that gentleman to single you out at the theatre," suggested Jane, in a diffident manner.

"Oh, one cannot gainsay Mr. Summers! Where he is concerned, I find myself doing all manner of things I had not previously intended."

Jane smiled: she could not think Celia serious.

"He is one of those irresistible charmers, is he?"

"He is such fun! And why should I not have a little fun now and then, pray—life with Francis is beyond anything dreary!"

Jane frowned. "If you find it so, why did you marry him?" she asked bluntly.

"My dear Jane, how can you ask? Who could refuse a Viscount who has the strongest expectation of soon becoming an Earl, and whose fortune, moreover, is as great as that of the Bordesleys?"

"I don't think such considerations should weigh at all," said Jane, indignantly. "Do you mean to tell me that you were never in love with him?"

Celia stared at her, then burst out laughing.

"Upon my word, you are an innocent!" she exclaimed. "Such romantic notions do not obtain in fashionable circles, let me tell you! Marriage is a matter of policy, for the most part—oh, yes, there is the odd love-match now and then, but most people find their amours outside marriage."

"If that is so," said Jane decidedly, "it is just as well that I don't belong to those elevated circles of which you speak. Such notions do not suit my way of thinking."

Celia looked amused. "I dare swear you believe in an undying love for one object, do you not?" she asked, mockingly.

Jane coloured a little, avoiding her eyes, but made no reply.

"I do believe you are already in love!" said Celia, watching her shrewdly. "Come, Jane, confess his name! Do I know him?"

Jane shook her head. "There is no one. Your imagination runs away with you."

"That I do not believe! But never fear, if he is one of our circle, I shall smoke him out! You had far better confide in me."

She waited a moment, but saw that she could expect no answer.

"Perhaps he is someone whom you have met in one of your posts," she went on, musingly. "Some tutor with a naughty eye, eh, Jane? Do you remember the dancing master at Miss Leasowe's? He was my very first conquest, and I was not then sixteen!"

"You quite mistake the matter. But since you are feeling more yourself, I will take my leave; it is getting late."

She said goodnight and returned to her own room, regretting the kindly impulse that had taken her into Celia's. It was plain to see that the girl had not changed from her schooldays. There was still the same lack of principle, the same disregard for anyone's feelings but her own. Almost Jane pitied the Earl, to whom she had taken an instant liking. But then, men of his age seemed to have a propensity for attaching themselves to women younger than they were; an attempt, perhaps, to recapture their lost youth. In the event, thought Jane grimly, he was more likely to find himself prematurely aged. However, it was no concern of hers. She dismissed the business from her mind, and prepared for bed.

She awoke the next morning to the comfort of a fire to dress by, and bright sunlight streaming across her bed through a window from which the abigail had drawn back the curtain. The girl returned presently with hot water, and a message from my lady to the effect that, if Miss Tarrant should care for it, she might partake of breakfast in my lady's boudoir. To such a civil request, Jane could only send back a polite acceptance, and in half an hour presented herself at Celia's door. On the threshold she paused, amazed at the sight that met her eyes.

The elegant room had been transformed into a bower of flowers. Huge baskets of daffodils, narcissi and softly coloured tulips stood about the room; while on every available small table were set bowls of violets and pale primroses.

Jane bent over the nearest of these, and gratefully inhaled the fresh, woodland scent.

"Wonderful!" she exclaimed. "Where did they all come from?"

Celia smiled complacently. "From Francis: this is his way of begging my pardon for his harsh treatment of me last night. Come and sit over here, and I will ring for the coffee."

The harsh treatment of which she spoke did not seem to have left its mark upon her this morning. She looked lovelier than ever in a peignoir of rose colour, which fell in soft folds about her. Jane, who was dressed in a morning gown of white muslin, felt suddenly out of place. In spite of all that the Spring flowers could do, the boudoir was for her too pampered a setting. She took a seat beside my lady at the low table before the fire.

"It is certainly a magnificent apology," she said.

Celia shrugged.

"I suppose so: everything that Francis does is on the grand scale, even his jealousy. You will see—for the next day or so, he will not be able to pay me too much attention. Pah, it sickens me! Let us talk of something else. I have an errand for you to undertake after breakfast—there is a note which must be delivered."

The meal over, Jane made herself ready to execute this commission. Celia placed the letter in her hand, enjoining her strictly to make haste and leave the house before Bordesley was astir, and that if there should be any reply to carry back, not to present her with it before the Earl's eyes. Jane did not much care for the scent of intrigue which this raised, but could not do other than concur.

As she left the house and descended the steps leading into the Square, she glanced at the direction written on the cover of the note. It was to a Sir Richard Carisbrooke, at an address in Brook St. Her heart missed a beat, for the name was familiar to her. Letitia Carisbrooke had been her dearest friend at school, and her home had been somewhere in Town. Could this Sir Richard possibly be some connection of Letty's? She very much hoped not, for it looked decidedly as though Celia were conducting some kind of illicit affaire with the gentleman concerned. Jane conceived an even greater dislike of her errand.

It was only a short way to the address, a typical Town house with a fanlight over the door and three stone steps leading down to the street. Jane raised the wrought iron knocker and tapped.

A manservant presented himself, and Jane explained her errand. The servant seemed uncertain what to do.

"Sir Richard is ill, madam," he said, hesitantly. "If you would like to see my lady, or Miss Letitia—"

"Oh, no," cut in Jane hastily. "It will not be necessary to disturb the ladies. If you will be good enough to ask one of them to deliver the note to Sir Richard when he shall have recovered—"

She broke off, as a young lady appeared in the hall, and seeing the door open, came forward.

"This lady has brought a note for Sir Richard, Miss Letitia," said the man, holding out Celia's letter to the newcomer.

The young lady, a merry-faced girl with dimples, blue eyes and yellow curls, looked first at the letter and then at Jane. What began as a casual glance turned into a long scrutiny. Recognition came into her eyes.

"Well, I never did! If it isn't my own Jane! You wretch, where have you been hiding yourself all these years? And why did you never write to me? Come in, come in; don't stand there upon the step! Mama will love to see you—I used to talk of you for ever!"

She seized the reluctant Jane by the arm, and ushered her through the hall and into a small drawingroom on the ground floor.

"Now we can talk!" she exclaimed, breathlessly; and proceeded to show her own ability in that direction. "Mama is upstairs with Richard—oh, Jane, are you acquainted with him? I did not know of it, but then, brothers can be sly when they choose! Green says you were leaving this note for him, so obviously you must be friends."

"No, Letty, you are mistaken," said Jane quickly, before her friend should have time to embark once more on a sea of words. "I am not acquainted with—your brother, is it?—I merely brought this note for him from Lady Bordesley."

Letty looked amazed and concerned. "Lady B— Celia Walbrook that was? Jane you are not—you cannot be staying with *her*? Why, you never liked her any more than the rest of us did! And if I thought that you were, after not even writing to me in all these years, why—why, I declare I would have done with you forever!"

Jane's worried expression gave pause to her friend's verbosity.

"No, Letty, I am not precisely staying there as a guest."

"You are in trouble, Jane, I know you are! I said so to Mama when you did not write after you left Miss Leasowe's. Jane, you must tell me—I insist. I may be able to help."

Jane saw that there was no help for it; she briefly explained the circumstances which led to her being in Celia Bordesley's household. Letty heard her out in a silence that was most unusual for her.

"A governess!" she exclaimed, when Jane had finished. "My dearest Jane!"

"A companion at the moment," corrected Jane, with a smile.

"And to Celia Bordesley!" said Letty, in tones of horror. "Oh, no, Jane, this must not be!"

"It is not so very bad," said her friend. "We manage tolerably well so far."

"But there must be something else to be done for you!" exclaimed Letty. "Your Papa—dear Jane, I was so distressed for you!—but he must surely have left you some money, and then you have relatives, I remember. Can you not make a home with any of them?"

Jane shook her head decidedly. "I have no fancy to be an encumbrance upon anyone. I am young, in good health, and like to be doing something, you know. At times the life is a little difficult, I will confess, but it has its compensations. I am constantly meeting new people, seeing fresh scenes; moreover, I am not obliged to be dependent upon anyone. That, to my mind, is the greatest evil that could befall me."

Letty was reluctant to believe that her friend could be happy in such a way of life, and put forward a number of wild schemes which should so much enrich Jane that she would no longer be obliged to earn a living. They both laughed heartily over these, and Jane promised to try them when all else failed.

"But why did you never write to me?" asked Letty, when they were sober again.

Jane glanced awkwardly at her friend, then looked quickly away.

"I—my circumstances were so changed—I did not wish to embarrass anyone; it seemed best to drop my former acquaintance."

"Jane Tarrant! How you could think—others, perhaps, but not I! After all that we had meant to each other—"

"Forgive me if you can, Letty. I never doubted your loyalty for one moment, but, indeed, it seemed the best way."

"Well, I fancy I know my Jane," said Letty, with a warm glance at her friend. "I'll say no more; but now that I have found you I shall hope to see a great deal of you. You are but a step away from us, after all."

"My time is not my own however," Jane reminded her.

"Oh, stuff! Celia Bordesley will be obliged to give you some time to yourself, and then you can spend it here with me. It will be quite delightful!"

Jane agreed, though with some mental reservations. She was very fond of Letty, and would have liked to resume their former friendship: but she could not help feeling the inequality of their respective situations, and wondered if perhaps Lady Carisbrooke would be as eager for the connection as her daughter. It was, after all, an age of snobbery.

"I am sorry that your brother should be unwell," said Jane, thinking to change the subject. "It is nothing serious, I trust?"

"We don't really know what has been the matter," replied Letty, with a worried frown. "The doctor himself is puzzled, but says it is some form of brain-fever. However, Riccy is better today; Mama has been able to talk to him for the first time, and he insists that he is quite able to get up. Jane, do you know what is in this letter? I'm not sure if it is wise to give it to him just yet."

"I'm afraid I cannot help you there."

Letty frowned at the note, which she still held in her hand.

"I'm certain that it can do him no good. Oh, I hate Celia Bordesley, I just hate her!"

Jane stared. Such an outburst of venom was unusual in her happy-go-lucky friend.

"Well, of course I know you never liked her. But what can she have done to give you such strong feelings?"

"It is on account of Richard!" choked Letty. "You cannot conceive what she has done to him! I tell you, Jane, he worshipped her—it was pitiful to watch. Why, on one occasion he almost cut Mr. Brummell himself, and I need not tell you what a social solecism that would have been! The poor boy thought that she meant to marry him, and when he found out that it was Bordesley, I shall never forget his face! And she led him on, Jane; it was deliberately done because she must have everyone admiring her, not because she really cared one jot for poor Richard! Knowing her as I do, I tried to warn him, but he would not listen. It is no use to try and tell men anything, my dear, though it should be staring them in the face. Always remember that!"

Jane promised gravely that she would, suppressing a desire to smile at the worldly-wise air which sat so oddly on Letty's dimpled face.

"I suppose I must give him this," continued Letty, reverting to the note. "But I shall wait a day or two, until he is really well, and so you may tell Celia. Oh, Jane, I hope she may not vent her spite on you! You must not stay there: why do you not come here? I know Mama would be pleased to have you for an indefinite stay, and as for myself—well, you know how I would feel, do you not? Do, please, leave that dreadful house, and come to us, dearest Jane!"

Jane was very firm in refusing this offer, while expressing her sense of Letty's goodness in making it.

"It is quite absurd that you should be reduced to such straits, Jane, when your father gave his life for his country! And there is Celia Walbrook, who is an undeserving character if ever I saw one, surrounded by every luxury; while you, who never did anything but good to anyone, have not a penny to bless yourself with!"

"Oh, Letty, come, it is not as bad as that!" Jane had to laugh at her friend's indignation. "As for Celia, believe me, I would not change places with her for all the Bordesley fortune," she added more soberly.

"No, I suppose not: but life often seems most unfair. Well, at any rate, you will be able to look in and see me pretty often. I would call on you, but that I must see her also if I do; and I've never yet bothered to call on Celia Bordesley, and don't mean to begin! You will come, won't you? And not let yourself be deterred by any of those silly notions of yours about putting upon people? 'Pon rep, Jane, you are the most independent, diffident girl I've ever met, and I love you for it, but I could sometimes shake you!"

Jane laughed and promised that she would indeed call when she should be free to do so. On this note, the two friends parted.

CHAPTER IX

RETURN OF THE STRANGER

DURING THE next few days, Jane had ample opportunity of observing the truth of Celia's prediction that the Earl would dance attendance on his wife. Indeed, Jane scarcely saw either of them. Bordesley bore Celia off to Bond St. in the afternoon of the day on which Jane had seen Letty, and they returned with a coach loaded with gowns and trinkets. The following morning, my lord drove Celia in the park arrayed in one of her new toilettes; in the evening, he accompanied her to a small private party where there was dancing. Jane found herself with a great deal of time on her hands, but she did not use it in visiting Letty, much as her inclinations ran that way. She did, however, pay a call on Mrs. Sharratt, who had expressed her desire of hearing how Jane went on in her new post. She was given a true account of the comforts provided, and the difficulties were glossed over. Thus Jane left the lawyer's wife with a comfortable feeling concerning her welfare.

After showing an initial annoyance at Jane's discreetly worded version of the message from Letty Carisbrooke, Celia had said no more of her delayed note to Sir Richard. Indeed, it had seemed to Jane that she betrayed a certain relief on hearing that the gentleman was ill. Perhaps, thought Jane, it was a connection which Celia began to find tedious; she hoped so, for Letty's sake.

Three or four days after his quarrel with Celia, the Earl began to revert to his custom of calling in at the clubs during the day, instead of accompanying his wife everywhere. Celia seemed not to mind this, actually expressing relief to Jane. "Nothing can be more tedious than having one's husband constantly at one's side!" she confessed. "Of course, it's very gratifying to have so many baubles given, but I'm not at all sure that it's worth the price of seeing no one but Francis for days on end."

This speech might have amazed Jane at one time; but a week in the Bordesley household had opened her eyes to marriage à la mode.

She and Celia were sitting together before the fire one morning, the Earl having left the house to meet one of his cronies, when a servant brought in a note for Celia. She glanced at the direction, then hastily tore it open. Its contents were short, but appeared to affect her powerfully. She jumped hastily to her feet, crumpled the letter and threw it on the fire.

"I have to go out at once, Jane!" she exclaimed. "If my lord should return in my absence, tell him I am gone to the Circulating Library—no, stay, you had better accompany me. I will leave a message for Francis with the porter."

Jane succeeded in understanding this speech better than it deserved. Evidently the note was responsible for Celia's urgent need of visiting the Library, and she was taking Jane along as a chaperone, hoping thereby to satisfy the Earl that her errand was harmless. Jane hoped that she might fulfil her part more successfully than she had done on the occasion of their visit to the play, and wondered what clandestine encounter she was now to be privileged to witness. Would it again be the debonair Mr. Summers?

She had no leisure to wonder for long, for Celia was in a fever to be gone; and many a slap did her abigail earn for dilatoriness, before my lady was ready to depart, a vision in dove-grey and pink. Celia had not summoned the carriage, a circumstance which confirmed Jane's suspicions about the nature of the errand. If my lady wished to be secret, she was wise not to travel in a vehicle which bore her husband's crest on its panels. The two of them therefore walked the short distance to the Library.

Once arrived, they found a number of people standing about the large room in little groups, some idly chatting in low tones, others taking down and scanning volumes from the shelves. My lady nodded to one and another, but passed purposefully on, refusing to be drawn into conversation; until she reached a doorway which led to a smaller, more secluded room. There was only one person here, a gentleman, his back towards them, making some show of glancing through the volumes on the shelves immediately before him. Jane saw that he was tall, with broad shoulders encased in a superbly cut coat, and thick dark hair, brushed in a casual style. Some premonition seized her, and she began to tremble.

The man turned at Celia's approach, and gave a curt bow. Jane looked full into his face, which was pale, with a suggestion of strain around the eyes.

It was the stranger from the Dartford road.

For a moment, she thought her senses would leave her. Every drop of blood seemed to ebb from her face, and she felt that the beating of her heart must be clearly audible to the others. There was a chair standing just a little way off: she groped her way there and sank thankfully on to it.

The gentleman glanced curiously at her, concern but no recognition in his look.

"Won't you go to your friend?" he asked Celia, in a low tone. "She looks as though she's about to swoon."

Celia threw an impatient glance behind her towards Jane.

"She certainly does look pale," she said wonderingly. "But she's not my friend, only a hired companion. I expect she'll be all right presently."

She turned her back on Jane. "Never mind about her!" she continued impatiently. "Tell me, Richard, have you got my letter? I could not understand your note—it put me in such alarm!"

"No, I have not," he answered ruefully.

"Not? But I don't understand—Julian said—"

"So you've seen Summers, have you?" he asked grimly.

"Yes, we met quite by chance at the theatre—and a fine scene Bordesley enacted me in consequence! But that is by the way. Julian gave me to understand that he had given you the letter in exchange for the packet I sent with you; and now you say you haven't got it, after all. Explain it to me, Richard, for I cannot make head or tail of it!"

"I'm damned if I understand the half of it myself," he answered, bringing his heavy brows down in a frown. "I certainly did see that scoundrel, and had the letter of him; and how I left him without putting a bullet through his false heart, I don't know. But you said no violence, so—" he broke off, with a helpless gesture of his hands.

"Yes, yes, but where is it?" hissed Celia, almost beside herself with anxiety. "If you had it then, you must have it now!"

He shook his head.

"This will sound odd, I know; it does even to myself. I had that letter of Summers, I put it in a secret place about me, and I rode off for London."

He broke off again, and looked through her into the middle distance.

"That much I remember clearly; and the next thing I remember is finding myself somewhere in a street down in the City with only a few shillings in my pocket, and all my possessions—wallet, watch, fobs, snuff box, quizzing glass— all gone!"

Celia stared at him for a moment without speaking; then an expression of contempt settled on her face.

"I wonder you should think to take me in with such a cock and bull story!"

"I know it does sound a trifle thin—that is why I have related it to no one else—but, believe it or not, it is the sober truth."

"Then you must have been in your cups!" exclaimed Celia, in disgust.

He shrugged. "I wish I could think so: any other explanation is too deuced creepy. But you might know I wouldn't drink with Summers; and as far as my recollection carries me, which is to within a mile or two of his place in Kent, I certainly didn't stop for refreshment. I set out from his house with the intention of pushing on back to Town in spite of the weather, for it had come on to snow when I arrived there. Believe it or not, Celia, the next thing I recollect is standing in this street in the City! I looked at a nearby clock, and it wanted a few minutes to one. I felt confoundedly shaky, and reached home I know not how. I believe you must know that I've been laid up ever since, for my sister babbled something about having sent you a message to that effect when your note was delivered at the house. They handed that to me only this morning; I replied at once."

"But this is fantastic!" exploded Celia.

He smiled mirthlessly. "I agree with you. However, I've been turning the business over in my mind, as you may imagine; and I fancy I've arrived at a possible explanation."

"I shall be glad to hear it," said Celia, in an acid tone. Julian's suggestion crossed her mind, and she wondered if there could be any truth in it.

"There's no doubt at all that I was robbed," he said. "Though why the thief should have had the mercy to leave me my fare home, passes comprehension! However, my medico said that he thought my recent malady might have been caused by a severe blow on the head; and it's just possible that such a blow would cause me to forget all that passed for a time afterwards. I didn't question him on the point, because obviously I'm not anxious to advertise the fact that I am unaware of my actions from close on six o'clock of one evening until the following afternoon—and I rely on you, Celia, not to spread such a tale abroad."

She gave him a scornful glance.

"I am not likely to do so; remember I have a stake in this affair! So you suppose that you were robbed? My letter would be taken with your other possessions, presumably, and therefore at this moment it may be anywhere. God, Richard, I cannot be easy until I have it in my hand! It spells my certain ruin if Francis should chance upon it! Is there nothing to be done to recover it?"

She seized his arm with these words, looking up imploringly into his face. He patted her hand reassuringly.

"Ah, but I think I know the identity of this robber, Celia. Never fear, I think we shall recover your letter!"

"What do you mean?" she asked, amazed.

"Who would be most likely to want to gain possession of that letter—who that knows of its existence, that is?" he countered.

A flash of illumination lit her face.

"You must mean Julian?"

She paused to consider the idea further, then shook her head.

"I don't believe it; he has a fondness for me, after all. I only half credited that he would indeed ever make use of the letter in the way that I feared, but you must realise that I could not afford to take a chance. I truly believe, knowing him as I do, that he would play fair, and relinquish all claim to the note once he had obtained his price."

It was his turn to look contemptuous.

"Upon my word, you have a very pretty idea of affection and fair dealing! I see now why I never made any headway with you!"

She gave him a guileless look from her deep blue eyes.

"What makes you think you did not?" she asked softly.

He held her glance for a moment, then his eyes flickered uneasily away from her face.

"Well, I persist in thinking that he has it," he said. "It all happened a deal too neatly for coincidence. It's my belief he gave that man of his—a shifty-eyed individual if I ever saw one!—the tip to lie in wait for me along my road home. I was admittted to the house by the fellow, but there was no sign of him when I left; and all along, I have had the oddest notion that he is in some way connected with this affair. I cannot positively say that I remember being set upon, but it is obvious that I must have been; granted that, I would be ready to believe that he was the man who did it. Call it an inner conviction, and sneer at it if you will, but it is nevertheless very strong."

"Can you really not remember being set upon?" asked Celia. "One would fancy you might at least recall that much."

He shook his head. "I remember perfectly riding off down the drive and through the gates of Farrowdene on my way back. It was snowing hard, and the wind was keen. I found it rough going along the lane which joins the house to the main coaching road, and my mare was picking her way like a cat."

He spoke slowly. It was evident that he was tracing the journey step by step in his mind.

"I turned into the main road, and we made better progress, though the snow was driving into my face so that I had my work cut out to see properly. I was thinking of that scoundrel I had left behind me, and of you, Celia—of the whole damned mess."

He broke off, and was silent for a space.

"That's all," he finished. "I've been over it many a time in my mind, and there is nothing more I can recall. It's as though I suddenly fell asleep there in the midst of it all."

There was a conviction in his voice that impressed even Celia's incredulity. She stared at him for a moment without speaking, then lightly shrugged her shoulders.

"You may be right; it is possible Julian has the letter. But why did he give me no hint of it when I saw him at the theatre?"

"Perhaps he means to wait a little," said Richard grimly, "until he has exhausted his ill-gotten profits. Then he will apply to you once more."

"I must say," said Celia, tartly, "you are both ready to believe the worst of each other. He suggested that you might be playing the same game."

"The damned scoundrel!"

"Perhaps; we shall soon know. I will ask him if he has it," said Celia, decisively.

His face hardened. "No, I'll do that. It will be a pleasure."

"Richard, I've told you before that you cannot call him out!" exclaimed Celia, laying a hand on his arm.

"We can find a good enough excuse. I don't care for his waistcoats—never have done, as a matter of fact!"

"Do you think anyone is deceived by such shifts? They have been smoked out before," replied Celia, scornfully. "And I won't take the chance of the affair coming to Bordesley's ears—I dare not!"

He reflected for a moment.

"There's only one thing for it, then!" he said. "To recover that letter in spite of Mr. Julian Summers."

"How will you set about that?" she asked, curiously.

"Quite simply: two can play at robbers, you know. If indeed it is robbery to seek to recover one's own property. It's not only your letter which the fellow has got, Celia, but everything that was in my pockets that day; including a watch given me by my father, and a snuff box which belonged to my grandfather. I'll be damned if I'll let him get away with it!"

"Servants can sometimes be bribed," said Celia, thoughtfully. "You mentioned Julian's man—I think I remember him, and, as you say, he looks none too honest. Why do you not approach him?"

"You may safely leave this to me," said Richard, guardedly. The idea of bribing a servant did not commend itself to him. "What I want to know is where I may see you in case of need."

"Francis will be away for a few nights, soon," replied Celia. "You may come as you did before. A note, or a word to my abigail first, just to make quite certain—"

An expression of distaste crossed his face.

"I mislike this hole and corner business, Celia! Are you quite sure that it's impossible to tell Bordesley the whole?"

"Are you mad? You must see that it is out of the question. We went through all this before, you may remember, and nothing has happened since to change the situation. Even now, I am foolish to be staying here all this time with you. That companion of mine may carry tales to Francis, for all I know."

Sir Richard glanced consideringly in Jane's direction.

"She has not the air of a person of that stamp. There is too much sweetness in the countenance. Have I encountered her before? There's something vaguely familiar about her."

"No, for she is but just arrived with us."

"Did I understand you to say as your hired companion? That is a new start, is it not?"

His tone was lightly contemptuous. Celia fired up.

"It is no notion of mine, but of Bordesley's! I don't want the silly chit, you may be sure! But I must go; if Francis should return, he will think it odd that I should be all this time at the Circulating Library. There is no bearing with his suspicions, I assure you!"

Her tone changed, and she placed her hand gently on his sleeve.

"Dear Richard; you are so good to me!"

He made no answer to this, but bowed and took his leave, moving quickly towards the door. As he passed Jane's chair, he inclined his head slightly with a smile: Jane returned the civility with as much composure as she could muster. It was evident that he did not recognise her.

When he had gone, Celia turned petulantly upon Jane.

"Upon my word, you look like a ghost! I only hope you do not mean to swoon, for I tell you plainly that I've no fancy to act the part of nurse! But perhaps you only meant to look pale and interesting in order to catch Sir Richard's eye: if so, you will no doubt be pleased to hear that he did remark your apparent indisposition."

"I believe I shall not swoon," answered Jane, with dignity. "And I must say that I have as little disposition to be nursed by you as you have for performing that office. I shall be perfectly myself again once we are in the fresh air."

At any other time, Celia might have taken up this speech; but she scarcely seemed to have heard it, having fallen into a fit of abstraction. In comparative silence, the two returned to Grosvenor Square.

Jane, too, had plenty to occupy her mind. For the rest of the day, she was hard put to it to keep her thoughts off the subject of the morning's encounter. As luck would have it, she was seldom alone; for once, Celia had no visitors or engagements, and Jane was constantly in attendance on her. It was a relief when at last she could shut her door of her bedchamber that night, and be alone to ponder the affair uninterrupted.

So the stranger she had met on the Dartford road was Sir Richard Carisbrooke, Letty's brother. And the letter which she and Mr. Sharratt had discovered in the snuff box, the letter signed with the initial "C", had obviously come from Celia. Jane recalled the wording of the letter—"F will be absent."

She gripped her hands tightly together. She had realised, of course, there in Mr. Sharratt's office, that the stranger she had met was in all probability conducting an illicit affaire with a married woman; but until now, she had not ceased to hope that there might be some possibility of error. She admitted this to herself at last, with a sense of loss such as she had not known since her father's death. She had agreed with her lawyer that it was best to forget, but all the time she had been building castles in the air. She had told herself that perhaps the liaison was an affair of the past, at present over and forgotten. Failing that, possibly the lady in the case was the victim of unhappy circumstances, a forlorn beauty in distress, tied to a coarse, brutal man.

An inward laugh of bitterness shook her at this recollection. Celia and the Earl of Bordesley? Such a description did not fit them! And how could she have been so foolish as to suppose that the man would save a letter to remind him of an affaire that was over? It was not a rational action: no, there could be no doubt that the man whom she had felt instinctively she could trust, to whom she had been so strangely, quickly drawn, was conducting a dishonourable affaire with my lady Bordesley. His meeting with her this morning, arranged so secretly, was the final proof.

She conjured up again, with some emotion, that same interview. She had not been close enough to hear anything of what passed, even if she had wished to do so; but every look, every gesture remained in her memory, and seemed in retrospect to speak of desire. At one point in the conversation, Celia had placed her hand upon Sir Richard's arm, and he had covered it with his; at another, they had shared a long, silent regard. His face had been turned in Jane's direction, though partly shielded from her view by Celia, so that she had been able to catch glimpses of his expression. It had been by turns grim, contemptuous and unhappy; very much as she remembered it on the journey in the stage coach to London, though now with the vagueness gone from the eyes.

It was plain to see that the connection with Celia had brought him nothing but unhappiness, as Letty had said.

A tumult of feeling rose within Jane. She longed passionately for the right to comfort him, shying away from the implications of her desire. She had not yet asked herself why she felt so strongly drawn towards this man; she only knew that she would have given all she possessed, little as it was, to see him safe from the torture that Celia evidently had the power to inflict on him. Her emotion at last overcame her, and she threw herself on to the bed, giving way to a torrent of weeping.

After a while, her sobs ceased, and she rose to bathe her eyes. She felt calm again; the tears, unusual with her, had acted as a safety valve for feelings which had been pent up for too long. Her reason once more took charge, and she asked herself what was to be done about the snuff box. Sir Richard ought to have it back; but how was this to be achieved without forcing herself on his notice? She inwardly flinched from the notion of explaining how she came by it; for it was evident that, with the recovery of his memory, he had lost all recollection of those hours with her in the inn and on the journey to London. It would be degrading, she thought, to accept his gratitude to a stranger, when she felt so much nearer to him than that.

No, she decided, she could not do it; not yet, at least. She would abide by Mr. Sharratt's advice, and leave the box where it was for the present. After all, it was perfectly safe. A little time might show her an easy solution to the problem. In the meantime, she must strive to banish its owner from her thoughts.

CHAPTER X

SIR RICHARD TURNS BURGLAR

WHEN SIR Richard Carisbrooke returned home from the Circulating Library, he found his sister sitting in one of the small salons, reading. She looked up as he entered, evidently pleased at the prospect of company, and threw down her book.

"I am glad you are come, Richard; I was longing for someone to talk to. How do you do this morning? You do not look at all the thing, let me tell you; your face is still as white as paper, and your eyes so dark, you would not believe!"

"I am well enough," he answered, impatiently. "What are you reading?"

He picked up the discarded book, hoping to turn the subject. Letty continued to speak of his health for some minutes, however, until he interrupted her with a question which she could not ignore.

"Did you not mention something the other day of a friend of yours in reduced circumstances who is acting as a hired companion to Celia Bordesley?"

"Oh, you mean Jane Tarrant?"

"Was that the name? I saw her this morning—although it has only just occurred to me who she must be."

"But how would you know her—oh, I suppose you mean to say that you saw her with Celia?"

He nodded.

A shadow crossed Letty's face.

"Richard, I do hope—you had that letter from Celia, and you went out directly—Riccy, she is not worth bothering your head about, really she is not, and I only hope you may not be such a gudgeon as to fall under her spell again!"

He eyed her warningly.

"You are a good creature, Letty, but you must allow me to manage my own affairs. This Miss Tarrant—is she as sweet as her countenance promises? She is a dainty little thing, is she not?"

"She not uncommon small," replied his sister, judicially. "But she is the dearest, sweetest girl in the world! I'll tell you something, Riccy, that I've not told to anyone save Mama. When I first went to school, I was feeling lonely and homesick—I dare say you know how it is, and I was not much above eleven, when all is said—anyway, I began to cry a little when I was left all alone with the others. One or two of them jeered at me for a cry-baby—your precious Celia amongst them—but Jane turned on them, and put a stop to it. Then, later, when we were all abed, and Miss Leasowe had put out the candles, I was sobbing quietly in my pillow, for I missed Mama and my own dear Nurse—you must know how it is, Riccy!"

He nodded gently. Such feelings were not confined to small girls, after all.

"Well, all at once, a hand crept into mine, and a voice whispered words of comfort in my ear. It was Jane; she must have stayed there until I slept, at the risk of a scolding if she had been caught, for the last thing I remembered in the morning was the warmth of her hand. After that, nothing seemed quite so bad; and of course, in a week or two, I was perfectly happy there. But I shall never forget that first night, and how Jane helped me to bear it."

"No," he answered gravely. "One could not forget a service of the kind."

He reflected for a moment, then asked, "What is her history?"

"I mentioned something of it the other day," said Letty, reproachfully. "However, I suppose you did not attend to me. Jane's father was a Captain in the Navy—a most handsome, dashing gentleman, who put all our hearts in a whirl whenever he came for her to Miss Leasowe's! He was killed in action, and she was left penniless, or as near to it as makes no matter. She disappeared abruptly from the Seminary, and no one ever heard from her again. Imagine my surprise when she called here with that letter from Celia! It seems that she has been earning her living as a governess ever since she vanished, and took this post with Celia because no others offered. Poor Jane! How uncomfortable a situation it must be for her!"

He frowned, and stood motionless, deep in thought.

"Yes, I suppose you must have told me, because now I

recollect the story vaguely. Are there no relatives to care for her?"

"Oh, yes, she has relatives, but I believe they are not wealthy. And if you knew Jane, you would realise how difficult it is to do anything to assist her. She is beyond all reason independent!"

"It does her credit," he replied absently.

He was silent awhile, then asked abruptly. "When you told me this story before, did you make any remark concerning her hair?"

Letty gazed at him in astonishment, weakly repeating his words.

He frowned again. "I only thought—there is something in my mind connected with such a comment—however, I may be mistaken. You chatter so much, my dear Letty, small wonder if sometimes I collect only a garbled version!"

This provocative speech could not be allowed to pass, and in the interchange which followed, Jane Tarrant's affairs were forgotten.

Darkness enshrouded the quiet Square. A pale, watery moon was veiled intermittently by grey clouds which scudded before the keen wind; the lights had been extinguished in the tall houses. A shadow deeper than the other shadows moved against the railings of one of the houses, and began to glide down the area steps. It halted before a small window which looked out on to the area. An interval passed.

The Watch, coming by that spot in his routine walk, paused and set down his lantern in order to adjust his muffler more securely against the wind. This accomplished to his satisfaction, he raised the lantern once more, and a chance ray discovered the man crouching at the window.

"Hey, there, what's toward?"

The Watch strode valiantly forward, cudgel raised.

The man at the window turned, revealing by the lantern's light the unmistakable countenance and apparel of a gentleman. He appeared quite unperturbed by the appearance of this custodian of the peace.

"Ah, perhaps you can assist me, officer! I find that I have left my key at home, and consequently cannot let myself in. My servants are all abed by my orders, and they must be astir early. It seems a pity on such a cold night to fetch them out. I thought it might be possible to get in by this window, but the sash-cord is gone; try as I will, I cannot make it stay open sufficiently to admit me. Now if you will have the infinite goodness to hold the thing up—"

There was a persuasive quality about the gentleman, and it was not such an unlikely tale. The Watch was perfectly ready to credit it, being familiar with the antics of the Quality in the small hours. He set down the lantern and cudgel, and obligingly held up the window frame. After much thrusting and squeezing, and a muttered oath at the sound of material being rent, the gentleman finally arrived at the inside. A hand came through the aperture with a clink of coin, and thanks were expressed in a low tone.

"Thankee, y'r honour!" replied the Watch, taking up his burdens of office and passing on his way. He reflected as he did so that it would be no bad thing if all the Quality were as thoughtful of their servants as this one.

Meanwhile, the gentleman groped his way through the room in total darkness, until he at last came to the door. Opening it, he found himself in a passage which he judged should run to the back of the house. In that quarter, if he was not mistaken, he should find a kitchen where a fire would still be burning, carefully damped down to last through the night.

It was as he supposed: he located the kitchen, and lit at the smouldering fire a portion of candle which he drew from the pocket of his breeches. Aided by the light of this, he began a cautious ascent of the stair.

He was by no means sure where to begin looking for what he sought, but the library seemed a more likely place than many. He found the room upon the ground floor at the back of the house. A three-branched candlestand stood upon the round mahogany table which was set in the centre of the room. He applied a light to the candles, and extinguished the one he was carrying, setting it down.

His eyes travelled round the room. Three of the walls were completely covered by bookshelves; the remaining wall was shared by a Gothic type bookcase with drawers beneath the glass-fronted cupboards, and a small rosewood bureau. With an air of satisfaction, he approached the latter, and hastily pulled down the top.

A jumble of papers met his gaze. He hesitated, as one who has no liking for his task; then squared his shoulders decisively, and lifted out a handful. He carried them over to the light, and began to flick impatiently through them.

'To 2 prs. Hessian boots with gold tassels—'

'To 6 dz. bottles Madeira—'

'To one coat in blue Superfine—'

He flung them down, taking another handful. These were couched in similar terms.

"Good God!" he muttered despairingly. "Does the fellow never pay any of his bills?"

He swept the papers impatiently aside, and delved into the pigeon-holes of the desk. Here he met with no better success. The entire bureau appeared to be given over to bills. He passed a hand distractedly through his thick, dark hair.

After a moment's hesitation, he turned his attention to the bookcase. Perhaps he would have better luck there. He pulled out the top drawer hurriedly, to be confronted once more with a miscellany of papers. He groaned, and bent over to examine them more closely.

At that moment, he heard the sound of the door-knob turning. He swung round quickly.

A man came into the room. He was clad in a handsome dressing gown of blue and gold brocade, and carried a lighted candle in his hand. This he proceeded to place upon the table in an unhurried manner.

"Good evening, Carisbrooke. I didn't apprehend that I was to have the pleasure of entertaining you, or you would have found me dressed. You must forgive me."

Sir Richard moved towards the table. He too, seemed quite unruffled.

"You must know why I am here," he said.

Julian Summers raised one eyebrow.

"You flatter my understanding, my dear fellow. You are badly dipped, perhaps, and thought to recoup some of your losses? Believe me, you've chosen the wrong place."

Sir Richard laughed shortly. "I came to recover my own property. Now that you are present, you can save me the search. Be good enough to hand me my wallet, watch and snuff box."

"Your —? My dear fellow, are you mad? But, of course, it is after two in the morning, when all is said; go home, my dear boy, and sleep it off."

Sir Richard's dark brows came down.

"I don't leave without my property, Summers."

The other man sighed.

"I see that this must be looked into," he said, but his eyes were wary, in spite of the weariness of his tone. "Will you take a glass of wine, Carisbrooke?"

"I want nothing, I thank you, but what I came for."

"Now I wonder why you should imagine that I have your—let me see, what was it?—ah, yes, your wallet, watch and snuff box, I believe. Do you seriously suppose, my dear chap—" he seated himself in an armchair, and indicated that his unexpected guest should do likewise "—that I have turned to petty larceny?"

"Oh, no," replied Sir Richard grimly, ignoring the invitation. "I do suppose, however, that you wished to retrieve Lady Bordesley's note."

"Ah, the fair Celia! So she comes into this. Perhaps you would not object to make things a little clearer, dear boy."

"I shall be happy," Sir Richard's mouth twisted ironically. "You may recall my recent visit to Kent, and the purpose for which I came?"

The other nodded, his light blue eyes fixed on his visitor's face.

"On my way home, I was robbed of all my possessions, including that note of Celia's. I believe, Summers, that it was one of your henchmen who did it, and at your instigation."

"Really?" Summers sounded amused. "But don't you know who did it, my dear fellow?"

A shadow crossed Sir Richard's face; Summers was quick to perceive it.

"I didn't see the fellow. But it's of no use to try and bluff me, Summers. You have that letter."

"And if I assure you that I have not?"

"What value is there in your assurance?" asked Sir Richard, scornfully.

The other shrugged. "As you please; nevertheless, it is a fact that I do not happen to be in possession of any of the missing articles."

For a moment, Sir Richard's resolution wavered. He had acted only on surmise in coming here to look for his property: what if Summers should be speaking the truth?

"Well, if you haven't got them, who the devil has? God knows where that note of Celia's may be at present!"

"Any ordinary pickpocket would make nothing of it," said Summers, consolingly.

"I felt convinced—what a damned blackguard you are, Summers, to put Celia in this coil!"

"She has put herself in it, has she not?" asked Summers, cooly.

"Damn you!" Sir Richard clenched his fists, and moved

threateningly towards the other man, who raised one arm protectively, and laughed.

"No, no, Carisbrooke, my dear fellow, everyone will tell you that I never fight. I do not pass my time, as you do, in sparring with members of the Fancy!"

"It might be better for everyone concerned if you did," replied Sir Richard, contemptuously. He stood looking down at Summers with eyes that smouldered, then suddenly shrugged, and cast himself into a chair.

"Come," said Summers, with a change of tone, "let us forget our differences for a time, and see if we can discover what all this is about. Where did you say you were set upon?"

Sir Richard hesitated. He did not wish to spread abroad the story of his loss of memory; he had already been obliged to confide it to Celia, and that was as far as he was prepared to go. His mind worked swiftly, accepting and discarding phrases.

"Within a mile or two of your house in Kent." He had been over this subject in his mind many a time, and it seemed to him that this must be the truth. Memory could carry him no farther, and a strong instinct insisted that the attack had taken place there. "I did not see my attacker, but I have an inner conviction that it was your man—I don't know the fellow's name. I remarked that when he admitted me to the house he eyed me strangely; and when I left, there was no sign of him. Thinking it all over since, I have come to the conclusion that you must have warned him to ride ahead and waylay me on my homeward journey, so that you might recover the letter."

He had taken a long chance, but it seemed to have come off: Summers' glance grew keen, and he straightened up in his chair.

"Perkins! Yes, b'God, I believe you are right! But you must take my word for it that there has been no conniving on my part. Celia had the letter of me in fair barter, and I had no more notion of taking it back again, than I had of purloining another man's trinkets."

He paused. Sir Richard did not interrupt, but watched his face closely.

"Perkins is enamoured of that slut, my lady's abigail," went on Summers, musingly. "I know from experience that the wench listens at doors. Could it be possible, Carisbrooke, that she overheard Celia telling you of this letter?"

Sir Richard started.

"I suppose it's always possible for servants to apply an ear to the keyhole if they're so minded. She certainly admitted me on the night that I visited Celia."

Summers nodded. "Then depend upon it, that is the explanation. She bears no love to my lady, I dare swear, and may have seen in this the chance to enrich herself at Celia's expense. Damme if I don't begin to think that I would have done better to have burnt that note! I seem to have helped kill the goose that lays the golden eggs."

Sir Richard gave him a look of deep contempt.

"You and my lady are a pretty pair, b'God! But you seem very ready to suspect this servant of yours—do you know him to be dishonest? Why not fetch him down and question him?"

"I have good enough reason for suspicion now that I have heard your story; and unhappily, I an unable to summon him. The fact is that I have not set eyes on Perkins since the moment of your arrival on that day. In a word, he has vanished."

CHAPTER XI

A CHANCE ENCOUNTER

"WHERE IS Miss Tarrant?" asked the Earl abruptly, coming into the boudoir on a morning two days later. He was wearing his driving coat, and carried a pair of tan leather gauntlets in his hand.

Celia looked up from a letter she was writing, faint surprise on her face.

"My dear Francis, how should I know? I sent her upon some errands an hour since—she should be back before long."

"Errands?" queried my lord sharply, frowning. "Surely the servants would more properly execute such trivial matters?"

Celia swung round in her chair, challenge in her blue eyes.

"We pay the girl's wages, do we not? That being so, it is fitting that she should earn them. I find it difficult enough to keep her employed as it is; if she is not to go upon an errand now and then, I wish you will tell me how she may be employed, for I am sure I can think of nothing."

"I meant her as a companion for you, Celia, not as an errand-girl. Will you please to make use of the abigails for such commissions in future?"

The Earl's tone was uncompromising. Celia took fire.

"It is time we made an end of this farce!" she cried, rising from her chair indignantly. "I have no need of a companion, and even supposing I had, I would never have chosen Jane Tarrant for the post! Upon my word, I cannot think what possessed you ever to hit upon such a notion!"

She paused for breath; he said nothing, but stood watching her, his eyes cold.

"I tell you what it is, my lord!" she went on, whipping herself up into a fury. "You may very soon find yourself choosing between us, for if she stays here, I shall not!"

As soon as she had uttered the words, she regretted them. Had she not determined to avoid admitting that she had noticed the Earl's interest in Jane? For once, her sense of drama had played her false: she must retract. But how? She studied his face. His expression was inscrutable.

"Is that an ultimatum?" he drawled.

"Nonsense!" she said, quickly. "All this fuss about a silly chit! I spoke but in anger; we are not to be quarrelling upon such a small matter, I trust. But you must allow me to find some employment for Jane—indeed, she herself does not care to be idle."

A sardonic smile curved his lips. For a moment, she felt that he could almost see into her thoughts.

"We will speak of this again," he said. "I am starting for Worcestershire at once, and expect to be absent some few days. I cannot be more definite at present."

"Again?" pouted Celia, once more mistress of herself. "I am for ever alone since you came into the title, Francis. Almost I think that it is not worth being a Countess to be obliged to part with one's husband so often!"

"Almost," echoed my lord, drawing on his gloves. "I imagine you might cheerfully sustain a great deal more inconvenience on that account."

"Cruel!" she answered, with a sob in her voice.

He caught her to him, pressing his lips fiercely on hers. She yielded, and for a moment they were locked together in a close embrace. At last, he raised his head, and looked searchingly into the hard blue eyes.

"Do you love me a little, I wonder?" he asked, softly; but it was as though he questioned himself.

"Dearest Francis, you know I do!" she replied in an intense tone which should have carried conviction. "Always we seem to quarrel over Jane Tarrant, but she is not worth it—nothing is, that can cause dissension between us! Do not be absent too long, my own, for I shall miss you so much!"

He released her abruptly, and taking his leave hastily, quitted the room. My lady stared after him for a moment; then, with a light shrug, settled once more to her writing.

Meanwhile, Jane Tarrant was walking homewards through the Park. It was a brisk morning, in spite of bright sunshine, and she stepped out in a lively manner, observing with pleasure all the signs of coming Spring. The grass was taking on that fresh hue which it wears in London only for a few short months of the year; there were buds on the black branches of the trees, and birds were singing. Life looked less dark than it had done on that evening two days since in her bedchamber: almost she felt happy, carefree. A song came to her lips.

A curricle pulled up beside her. She looked up, and the song died away.

"Miss Tarrant, is it not?"

The gentleman who was driving removed his hat, allowing the breeze to disorder his thick, dark hair.

"My name is Carisbrooke; I believe you are acquainted with my sister. Can I have the pleasure of driving you anywhere, madam?"

For a moment, Jane was unable to speak. During the last few days, she had succeeded in banishing all thoughts of this man, and recapturing her usually sanguine frame of mind. His sudden appearance brought back the past. She clasped her hands firmly together in the obscurity of the muff which she carried, and tried to speak lightly.

"How do you do, Sir Richard? I believe I need not put you to so much trouble. I have but a step to go, and am enjoying the walk."

"I assure you there is no trouble in the case," he asserted, swiftly. "You are bound for Grosvenor Square, I collect? It lies in my way."

With a quick flick of his wrists, he gave the reins into the keeping of the stable-lad who rode behind him, and vaulted down. His hand was under her arm, and she was up in the seat beside him before she could open her mouth to protest.

"A pleasant morning," he said conversationally, as he once more took the reins, and the vehicle started forward.

Jane agreed in an absent tone. She was conscious of a slight feeling of indignation. She had determined to put this man out of her thoughts, and had been succeeding tolerably well. Why, then, must a perverse fate make him choose to force his company upon her?

"Are you usually so overbearing, sir?" she asked, with a smile which robbed the remark of any offence.

He threw her a startled glance, then laughed.

"Am I? Why do you say so?"

"Because you chose to ignore my refusal of your kind offer."

He shrugged, his eyes twinkling. "My sister tells me that you are the most difficult person in the world to persuade to accept a service. I thought to save my breath."

"Dear Letty!" Jane's smile was affectionate. "But you cannot believe all she tells you of me; she is too partial an observer. Truly, I was enjoying my walk. It is such a lovely morning."

"Then perhaps after all I had better set you down again?" he asked teasingly, making as if to rein in the horses.

"On no account," she replied in the same vein. "Since you have been put to the trouble of getting me up here, the least I can fairly do is to stay until we reach the Square."

He bowed ironically, and for a moment his dark eyes rested on her face. Jane lowered her glance. She felt very conscious of his presence, the more so because there was not much room on the seat of the curricle, and occasionally their elbows touched. She was determined, however, not to allow him to overset her composure, and to treat him exactly as she would any other gentleman of her acquaintance whom she might have chanced upon in the Park. She began to speak of the weather, discussing the dilatoriness of Spring.

He replied absently to her remarks, though he seemed to be listening intently enough. Presently he interrupted her abruptly.

"You have a pleasant voice, Miss Tarrant. Where have I heard it before this?"

With difficulty, Jane suppressed a start. Could it be possible that he was beginning to remember? She was uncertain what answer to make, and therefore kept silent.

"You may perhaps have visited with us when you were at school with my sister?" he persisted. "It is unpardonable of me to have forgotten, I confess, but—"

Jane shook her head. "No, I was never at your home. Not for lack of invitations, however."

He sighed. "No? Well, I suppose I must have imagined it—" he broke off; after a moment's pause continuing— "Speaking of invitations, are you at liberty to call upon my sister this morning? Nothing could give her greater pleasure, I know, and I will gladly take you there if you but say the word."

Jane knew a moment's regret. So he did not remember, after all. Perhaps it was as well, she reflected: she had no wish to be an object of gratitude to him. Somehow a way must be found to return the snuff box without ever allowing him to guess her part in the affair. She would speak to Mr. Sharratt about it. She dismissed the thought hastily, and replied to his question.

"I am very sorry, but it is quite out of my power at

present. I've already been absent some time, and my lady Bordesley—"

"She, too, was a schoolfellow of yours, was she not?" he asked, quickly.

She assented, a certain resentment rising within her. Mention of Celia recalled the meeting in the Circulating Library, and her own unhappiness following it. She did not wish to dwell on that.

He glanced swiftly into her face.

"I am sorry," he said, awkwardly. "Your situation cannot be a happy one—"

He broke off, evidently embarrassed.

"I imagine," he went on, after a pause, "that you could not have been aware when you accepted the post, that you were to come to an old schoolfellow?"

Jane shook her head.

He glanced at her again, seemed about to speak, then changed his mind. For a few moments, he appeared to be labouring under some inner conflict. At last, he burst out, "You ought not to be there!"

Amazement showed momentarily on Jane's face.

"Why not?"

"Celia Bordesley is no fitting companion for a young lady such as you!" he said vehemently, as though the words were torn from him.

Jane raised her brows. She turned to face him, a challenge in her grey eyes.

"Yet she is a friend of yours," she stated calmly.

"That is different," he answered curtly.

"I do not see why." Jane was coldly obtuse, but her heart was beating fast. Why should he show this sudden, almost impertinent interest in her concerns?

"I have been about the world a little," he answered, impatiently, "and, moreover—but my dear Miss Tarrant, this is absurd! You must see that there can be no parallel between the two cases."

She decided that it was high time to introduce a lighter note to the conversation. They were getting into deep waters.

"So I am absurd, am I?" she asked, tilting her chin. "I thank you, sir!"

"Forgive me," he answered, impetuously. "I had no right—I should not have spoken as I did—"

He broke off, and glanced sharply at her too demure countenance.

"I do believe you are roasting me!" he accused. " 'Pon my word, it's too bad of you!"

Jane laughed, revealing an unexpected dimple.

"We cannot be quarrelling, Sir Richard, without even the benefit of a formal introduction. Say no more on the subject, and let us be friends."

His dark eyes held hers for a moment, and a frown creased his brows.

"It is impossible!" he said, softly.

"That we should be friends?" she asked, teasingly.

"No, not that, of course! But that we should not have met before—"

He stopped, and looked earnestly into her face. She coloured, and turned her eyes away.

"In any event, I am arrived at my destination. I must thank you, sir, for a pleasant ride."

He looked up, and saw that they had indeed arrived at the entrance to the Square.

"I will take you directly to the door," he said.

"No," Jane answered quickly. "If you will be so good as to set me down here—"

He saw that she did not wish him to be observed taking her home, and did not persist. He jumped down, and assisted her to alight. Her colour was heightened, and she avoided his eyes, but she bade him goodbye calmly enough, and sent a message for Letty.

After she left him, he stood still in the road for a minute or two, looking after her, his dark brows down in a puzzled frown. The fidgeting of the horses and a faint cough from the stable-lad recalled him at last to his surroundings; he swung himself back into his seat and once more took up the reins.

CHAPTER XII

UNACCOUNTABLE

BEHAVIOUR OF MY LORD

LADY BORDESLEY yawned, and stretched herself with the lazy grace of a cat. She glanced at Jane, who was sitting on the opposite side of the fire, busily plying her needle at a cushion-cover of which my lady had tired.

"God, I'm bored! Do you not find life inexpressibly dull, Jane?"

The other looked up for a moment from her work, holding the needle poised.

"Not dull, precisely; no, never dull. There are too many variations for that, don't you agree?"

"I cannot think why you, of all people, shouldn't find it so," remarked Celia, with a touch of malice.

"Why myself more than another?" enquired Jane, going on with her task.

"Obliged always to be at the beck and call of others, never to have anything exciting happen to you; always to be dressed in the cheapest clothes—to pinch and scrape, to smile and make the best of it—bah! I tell you, it would drive me so distracted I should most likely put poison in the milk of my charges, or scratch out my employer's eyes!"

She put so much expression into her face whilst uttering these words, that Jane was constrained to laugh.

"It's fortunate, then, that these things have fallen to my lot rather than yours. But truly, Celia, you dramatise my life; it is not so very bad. Sometimes, perhaps, I am not quite content. For instance, I must confess to a fondness for pretty clothes that so far I've not been able to gratify. But you're mistaken when you say that nothing exciting ever happens to me; things of that kind are happening all the time to everyone, in all walks of life. In any case, you are possessed of all

93

those things which you say I lack: do you find yourself any happier, or less bored on that account?"

Celia stared, then burst out laughing.

"Oh, well done, Jane! Touché! I suppose I am not. Oh, I'm happy enough at a grand Assembly, or when I have a new gown; but for the most part, my life is insipid, tedious!"

Jane set a stitch carefully before replying.

"Perhaps that might be because you have never learnt to centre it on another," she said.

Celia's lips twisted.

"True love, again? Come, Jane, who is this man? For I'm convinced there is one!"

Jane kept her head bent over her work, but made no answer.

"I wonder now," said Celia, musingly, "why you were so overcome in the Circulating Library the other day? Did you see him there, by any chance?"

"It was close in there after the cool air of the street," replied Jane, as carelessly as she was able. "I am often similarly afflicted in hot rooms."

"I haven't before observed it," said Celia, eyeing her narrowly. "Let me see, now, whom did we pass on our way in? They were mostly females, if my recollection serves me rightly. Oh, there was Mr. Verrett, of course, with that silly sister of his—could it be he, Jane? But surely not; he is obese, and has a squint in one eye! Lord Symmons, then: it is no use to set your cap at him, Jane, for he is married already, and has a daughter older than you. Of course, a liaison is always possible, but I do not much fancy your chances beside an Opera dancer. One could not precisely call you a little bit of muslin, you know, and men prefer their pastimes to be empty of head and morals alike. Your worst enemy could not say that of you; perhaps that is what makes you so inordinately dull!"

Jane lifted her head, and fixed the other with her candid grey eyes. She was prepared to carry the war into the enemy's camp.

"Have you ever been in love, Celia, I wonder—really in love, so that you cared for the object of your affection more than for yourself?"

"A fool's question, Jane. I told you once before that it is folly to love in that way. I have been in love a dozen times, but only as much as it pleased me. Take my advice, and follow my example. Why, if you choose, you might lead a very different sort of life, for I must say that you are not bad-looking, Jane."

"I thank you," replied Jane drily, and was silent for a while.

She threaded her needle with a strand of red silk, and set the first stitch in a rosebud on the design. Her thoughts were busy; there was something she was determined to find out if she could.

"But surely there must have been someone," she persisted, looking up suddenly into Celia's face. "Someone who meant more to you than the rest? That gentleman we met at the theatre, for example, or—or Sir Richard Carisbrooke?"

The name came out more easily than she would have believed possible.

"Julian," said Celia, softly. "Yes, I think if I could love any man in the way that you mean, Jane, it would be he. But much I should get for my pains! No, we understand each other too well to harbour any such romantical notions. As for Richard—"

She paused, and a slight frown creased her brows.

"I used to think of Richard as a dear, ingenuous boy. He is changed, though, in these four years—that swift, imperious manner is new to him, and there is a cynical air, very different from what I remember, and vastly fetching! But as for anything in the nature of your undying passion, Jane, I am afraid it would never be he who had the power to raise it. No, Richard is intriguing, and it might be sport to bring him to my feet again, but that is all."

And more than enough, thought Jane. So complete an avowal of Celia's intentions was unexpected, but the content was exactly as Jane had supposed. She pressed her lips together to still the trembling which suddenly overcame them, and wondered what the man's feelings might be. Presumably he still found Celia irresistible, since he sought clandestine meetings with her. Yet Celia had spoken as though she had lost him, if not irretrievably; and surely if he were in love with her, he could not have spoken of her as he had done in the Park yesterday morning? He had said that she was no fit companion for Jane. These were not the words of a lover.

Celia broke in suddenly upon these reflections.

"By the way, Jane, I meant to ask this of you the other day—do not mention to my husband that I met Richard in the Library."

Jane's glance was indignant.

"Do you suppose that I should?"

Celia shrugged. "Why not? I tell you plainly that I suppose Francis to have brought you here for that purpose: presumably you are bound to do that for which you are paid."

"No such undertaking," said Jane, with emphasis, "was ever given by me—or indeed, sought. I came here as your companion, no more."

"There is one other possibility," said Celia, eyeing Jane narrowly.

"And that is—?"

"Could it be my lord who inspires in you these feelings of high and noble love?" asked Celia, quickly.

Jane stared at her for a moment, then gave a short laugh.

"Why on earth should you suppose so?"

The incredulity in her tone satisfied my lady. Jane, she was prepared to swear, was no actress.

"Just a notion I had," she said. "I see I was wrong."

She did not mean to put ideas into the other's head by explaining that she had noticed a certain interest, a warmth in the Earl's manner towards his wife's companion. Celia would have found it difficult to believe that a girl in Jane's situation would not hasten to ingratiate herself with the Earl, should she have reason to belive that there existed any partiality on his side. She therefore said no more, and a silence fell for some moments, during which Jane was free to pursue her own thoughts.

These were not altogether agreeable. She was recalling an incident brought to mind again by what Celia had just said, an incident concerning the Earl. It had occurred a few days ago, before the Earl's departure for Worcestershire. Lady Breakwell had been sitting with Celia at the time, and Jane had been peremptorily dismissed. She had drifted into the drawing room and seated herself at the pianoforte, idly strumming as the fancy moved her. At such moments, alone and immersed in the memories recalled by the music she was playing, she was apt to be a little off her guard. Thus it was that she suddenly looked up with eyes luminuous with unshed tears, to see the Earl of Bordesley standing beside her chair.

She could not realise what a bewitching picture she presented. The soft candlelight imparted a golden glow to the skin of her shoulders, partly revealed by the neckline of the simple yellow gown she wore; and her hair glinted with fiery lights as she moved her head.

He looked down at her with a glance that startled Jane by its warmth.

"The golden girl," he said, softly.

She rose hastily, the colour mounting to her cheeks.

"No, do not stop." He arrested her movement with a gesture of his hand. "Will you be good enough to play that air for me again?"

Jane complied, her fingers stumbling slightly. It was an old English air that had been a favourite of her father's. The Earl placed one hand upon the instrument, and stood listening in silence until she had finished.

"Thank you, Jane," he said, quietly. "You do not mind if I call you Jane, as my wife does?"

Jane inclined her head stiffly. She did mind, very much, and made a mental note to call tomorrow at one of the employment agencies.

"My mother was very fond of that air," continued the Earl, reminiscently. "You remind me of her."

This was a gambit to which Jane was not unused. In spite of her efforts to subdue her good looks, there had been one or two occasions in her career when her virtue had been attempted. Such incidents had always involved finding a fresh post. She sighed; she had thought herself free here from that kind of happening, at least. All her anxieties had been on Celia's account. It was never the hazards one forsees, she reflected, with a tinge of bitterness.

Aloud she said, "Your lordship will please to excuse me; there are commissions I must execute on my lady's behalf."

She half rose as she spoke; but he placed a beringed white hand on her shoulder, gently pushing her back into her seat. His green eyes held an inscrutable expression.

"There is no need of haste, my dear young lady."

He paused, and looked down into her eyes, his hand still on her shoulder.

"You are wise beyond your years, Jane. What do you think of my marriage?"

Jane started, and returned his glance coldly.

"It is not my affair to think of such matters, my lord."

He dropped his hand, as though for the first time he realised the implication she might place upon his words and actions.

"What you say is very proper; would to God my lady might have such a nice sense of propriety! But it is not proper sentiments I want from you, Jane, but the truth:

those eyes, I dare swear—" he placed his fingers beneath her chin, tilting up her head—"cannot lie. Tell me truly, Jane, is not my marriage a mistake?"

For a moment, in spite of herself, Jane felt a strange affinity flow between them. She put away his hand with fingers that were not quite steady, and lowered her gaze.

"You have answered me, though you never spoke a word," said the Earl. "Yes, I myself know it is a mistake. There is no real understanding between Celia and myself; I should never have married her."

Again, this speech held a familiar ring. Jane had before this encountered gentlemen whose wives, according to their report, did not understand them. Her chin went up, and she rose in a decisive manner.

"I can no longer listen to you, my lord," she said, with a quelling glance. "You wrong all of us by such talk—your wife, yourself, even me."

His countenance filled with dismay, and he started forward: but she swept quickly from the room, closing the door firmly behind her. He did not follow.

Sitting now beside Celia, Jane relived this incident in her mind. She had forgotten it in the distraction of yesterday's meeting with Sir Richard, but reviewing it now, in the light of what Celia had just let fall, it was distinctly disquieting. Perhaps she had made a mistake in changing her hair from its once severe, repelling style; but after the remarks made by—by someone who should be nameless, the urge had come over her once more to make herself as attractive as Nature had intended her to be. Evidently she must have succeeded only too well. She frowned; yet the Earl's manner could not definitely be considered amorous. Was it perhaps his own particular technique in the business of seduction? His words, she reflected, were almost exactly the same as those in which her favours had been sought on previous occasions.

She shrugged her shoulders slightly, a sinking feeling at her heart. There was no profit in thinking further of the matter. There were many matters of which she must not think ...

Celia yawned again, more widely, but still daintily.

"Come, Jane, we will retire early," she said, glancing at the clock. "Time hangs so heavily without company, and with Francis absent from home, there is no occasion to keep the servants up."

This speech had the effect of bringing Jane out of her reverie. It was a novel idea for my lady to consider her servants.

"Heigh ho!" said Celia, rising and extending her white arms above her head in a luxurious stretching gesture. "I declare one becomes more fatigued sitting quietly at home than dancing half into the night! But it is ever so; it is always the tedious things which quite wear one out."

CHAPTER XIII

WITHOUT RHYME OR REASON

JANE LINGERED before the fire in her bedchamber, unwilling to begin preparations for bed. Sleep could not be wooed with an unquiet mind, and her mood at present was very far from tranquil. She rested her chin in her hands, and idly watched the reflection of the leaping flames in the smooth polished surface of the bed-post.

It began to look as though she could no longer stay in this house. She had feared from the first that it might be so, but for the wrong reasons. The disadvantages which she had foreseen paled before those which had come unexpectedly upon her. The fact that she disliked Celia, the occasional outbursts of spite which the other showed to her, were things tolerably easy to endure: she had met such difficulties before, and found that they yielded to a cheerful disposition. But the Earl's apparently growing interest in her was quite another matter. Her experience had taught her that in affairs of that kind the best course to pursue was to go before it was too late. A girl with neither fortune nor connections could not hope to preserve her good name if she remained in the house of a wealthy nobleman who had taken a fancy to her.

She sighed: the one great difficulty of her situation was that she had nowhere to go. This obstacle was always present, the necessity of finding a fresh post before she could quit the old one. She had that morning called at the employment agency, only to be told that there was nothing available at the moment. They had promised to inform her when a suitable post offered. There was nothing more she could do. She must remain here for a time, at any rate; if the situation became too desperate, she could always go to the Sharratt's. It was a measure she did not care to adopt unless no other possible course was open to her, but at least it was there, a final refuge.

She frowned a little as she recalled that Mr. Sharrat had

shown some doubt when he had learned the name of her new employer. What exactly was it that he had said? Could he have had any suspicion, have heard any rumour concerning the Earl's reputation? The lawyer was not the man to take alarm without sound reason, Jane knew.

And even this was not the worst. If she remained here, she must risk the chance of encountering Sir Richard Carisbrooke. Her friendship with his sister must inevitably lead her into this hazard, even if he came no more to see Celia. Jane confessed to herself that she could not continue to meet him with equanimity. She had succeeded tolerably well so far in putting him out of her thoughts. The encounter of yesterday morning had again overset her feelings for a time. It would not do: it would be best to go away, go to some place where their paths would never again cross.

She rose impatiently, unwilling to pursue her thoughts further. She determined to read for a while; had it been daytime, a walk would no doubt have helped to shake off her introspection. At this hour, a book offered her only hope of escape from her own concerns.

She rose, and crossed over to the table at her bedside, taking up the book which lay there. As she did so, she realised with annoyance that she had already finished it. She paused irresolutely for a moment. There would probably be something or other suitable downstairs in the library. Was it worth the trouble of the journey?

Eventually, she decided that it was; sleep seemed as far away as ever. She took up the candle from her table, and lit it at the fire.

She passed quietly from her bedchamber, so as not to disturb Celia. There was no sound from the other's room, and the house seemed deserted. Most likely the servants were already abed. Her light slippers made no noise as she glided quickly down the staircase, the flame of the candle dipping with the draught of her movement. The large hall with its chequer-board floor was cold and dark. She shivered as she crossed it, and came at last to the library.

She entered, closing the door silently after her. There were a number of candelabra set about the room at intervals, and she lit one or two of these from her candle. The room wore a gloomy, musty aspect, as though it were not much used. She had never been here before, and decided that, when next she came, it would be in daylight. The place looked singularly uninviting by night.

She conquered her feelings, setting down her candle and beginning her search. She soon despaired of finding a novel; no wonder Celia preferred the Circulating Library. Here were volumes of sermons, the Greek and Latin poets, and heavy tomes which would have been an encumbrance to convey upstairs. Her eye lighted upon two such volumes, entitled "Animated Nature." Curiosity impelled her to pull one of them forth from its place on the shelf. She saw that the work was written by Oliver Goldsmith, and had been well-thumbed. She placed the heavy book upon the table, and idly flicked over the leaves.

It was such a book as might appeal to a child, dealing as it did with animals. Her quick imagination conjured up the image of a child standing here as she was doing, turning these pages with fingers that were not always, as the evidence suggested, quite clean. She smiled at her fancy, and turned another page. As she did so, a paper fluttered to the floor.

She bent to retrieve it, and was about to place it once more in the book, when she saw that it was the likeness of a young girl. She brought her candle nearer, and inspected the drawing closely. The colours had faded a little with age, but the unknown artist had caught something of the spirit of his subject, for the face seemed to live. It was pointed, elfin, surrounded by auburn curls; the green eyes danced and laughed, as though their owner found life a merry business.

Jane frowned; surely that face was familiar to her? Then she noticed the name painted in at the foot of the drawing— Arabella Bordesley. So that was the explanation; this was a relative of the Earl's, his sister or his mother. Judging by the style of the gown, Jane thought it more likely to be his sister.

She gazed with a new interest. Evidently the young Arabella had been a lively, merry girl, with more than her share of good looks. Jane wondered idly what differences time might have wrought in her. Strange that this sketch, which surely must have been accounted good by even the most partial of observers, should have been allowed to lie forgotten in a book. One would have expected to see it hanging on a wall in one of the principal rooms. Now that she came to consider it, Jane did not recollect having seen any other pictures of the lady about the house. Was this deliberate, she wondered, and if so, was it the Earl's doing, or Celia's?

Unaccountably, she shivered. She told herself that it was cold here in this large fireless room. She gave one last look at the portrait, then replaced it in the book with gentle fingers, as though she laid a child to sleep. Impatient now to be gone, she hurriedly replaced the book on its shelf, and seized the first slim volume which came to hand, an edition of Cowper's poems. Taking up her candle, she extinguished the others, and quitted the room.

She was halfway up the staircase on her return journey to her bedchamber, when she fancied she heard a sound. She stood still, listening. The eerie quiet of a house at night, when everyone is abed, closed all around her, seeming to press on her ears. Only the loud beating of her heart broke the silence.

Stay, there it was again; a muffled, regular sound overhead, of footsteps stealthily approaching from the other side of the house, in the direction of the servant's staircase. For a moment, she was unable to move.

She told herself impatiently that she must not be nonsensical. No doubt it was one of the servants still astir, creeping about quietly to avoid rousing the rest of the household. She forced herself to continue on her way, climbing the rest of the stairs with slow, reluctant steps. As she mounted higher, the mysterious footsteps drew nearer to the landing which was also her objective. There could now be no doubt that when she reached the head of the stiarcase, she would encounter someone.

She squared her shoulders: she must not give way to idle fancies. It would be only one of the servants.

Her foot was on the topmost stair, when she perceived two forms approaching her from the passage on her left. Relief flooded over her as she recognised the one carrying the candle. It was Betty, Celia's abigail. Her companion was a man, but she could not determine his identity, as his face was in shadow. She waited uncertainly for them to come up to her.

All at once, she dropped her candlestick with a clatter. Vaguely, she felt the hot wax run over her hand, as the candle extinguished itself in the fall.

The man at Betty's side was Sir Richard Carisbrooke.

He looked in quick surprise at her white, strained face.

"Miss Tarrant!" he exclaimed, in a low tone, and stood quite motionless for a moment, regarding her in dismay. Then recollecting himself:—"I have given you a shock, madam, I fear; no wonder. Seeing me approach thus quietly, you must have thought me an intruder. I beg your pardon."

He stooped to pick up the fallen candlestick, and placed it into Jane's nerveless hand. He turned to the abigail.

"Betty, see Miss Tarrant to her room. I will find my own way."

"Will you bring all the house about us, y'r honour?" asked Betty, in a furious whisper.

"I have no need of assistance, I thank you, sir," replied Jane, still pale, but now composed. "It was just that I was not expecting to meet anyone here and at this hour."

For a moment longer, he stood looking at her as though lost to all sense of urgency; then he seemed to collect himself, and a shade of embarrassment crept into his manner.

"If you are quite sure—"

"Perfectly, I thank you. Goodnight," answered Jane, shortly.

Still he lingered irresolutely, until an impatient movement from Betty recalled him to the purpose of his presence there. Reluctantly, he accepted his dismissal.

"Goodnight, Miss Tarrant."

He and the abigail continued on their way, and after a moment's hesitation, Jane followed them. It was an unlucky chance that her room should be next to Celia's, that she should be obliged to watch this man going to his mistress. Her heart swelled, and a burning anger seized her. She hated Sir Richard Carisbrooke—hated him! Had he not spoken yesterday as though he despised Celia? Yet here he was, going to her room when her husband was from home, creeping furtively by way of the servants' staircase to keep a dishonourable appointment! And this was the man—

Her train of thought broke off, shattered by the words she had been about to use. A flood of illumination swept over her. At last she knew the truth. She did not hate Sir Richard: this was the man she loved.

She closed the door of her bedchamber, and stood motionless behind it. This could not be true, there must be some mistake. Her imagination—she had always been possessed of a lively imagination, she knew—must have misled her. Jane had thought sometimes of love, as what girl does not? Love for her was to be a slow, ripening process, the fruit of many meetings and mutual interests. She had never believed in love at first sight. That surely, she told herself, was an invention of novelists, whose business it was to make everything slightly larger than life. Her reason strove against her conviction, but in vain. However unreasonable, almost impossible, it might be, the fact was that she did love Sir Richard.

She pressed her hands to her breast, as though by that

means she could still the tumultuous beating of her heart. What was to be done? Her case was hopeless; he felt nothing for her but a kindly interest, no doubt aroused by Letty's reminiscences of their schooldays. It was Celia who filled his thoughts, Celia, who at this very minute, doubtless, was clasped to his heart.

If only Celia had cared for him! It would still have been wrong, a betrayal of the Earl, but at least it would have been understandable. But by her own avowal, made this very evening, she sought only to amuse herself in making a conquest of him.

She must not, shall not succeed, thought Jane desperately; somehow, a way must be found to prevent her. But how? Celia had everything to aid her purpose, beauty, wealth, and a supreme indifference to the feelings of others. What weapons had Jane Tarrant with which to fight her?

What weapons? Why, there was the letter. The thought came to her with a suddenness that made her catch her breath. If she were to take the letter to the Earl, that would put an end to Celia's amorous exploits. He would most likely divorce her, at the very least curtail her liberty. In either event, she would be too taken up with her own concerns to bother about the conquest of one to whom she was in reality indifferent. Sir Richard would be safe from her.

But no! He could no more be safe than she, Jane, could be safe from a hopeless love. Whether or not Celia wanted or encouraged him, he would still love her because he must. In love there was neither rhyme nor reason, as Jane had good cause to know.

Her honesty compelled her to examine again her motive for considering such a course as taking the letter to my lord. Had she really thought that she could thus save Sir Richard from his entanglement?

She shook her head sadly. No; another motive lay hidden behind this urge. The unpalatable truth was—she faced it squarely—that she sought revenge on the woman who had killed all hope of her ever possessing the man she loved.

The acknowledgement of this did much to restore her calm. An instinct for revenge might be one of the most natural of human emotions, but Jane was not the person to indulge it. Nevertheless, she had to struggle against the temptation, and, in overthrowing it, she also got the better of the wave of intense feeling which had tormented her for the past ten minutes.

Drained of emotion, at last she could sleep. She moved towards the dressing-table, putting up her hands to unfasten from her neck the locket which she always wore, a locket containing her father's picture.

She was arrested in the movement by a loud hammering upon her door, and Celia's voice crying in sharp accents, "Jane, Jane, come quickly!"

CHAPTER XIV

AN EVENTFUL RENDEZVOUS

AFTER SIR Richard left Jane at the head of the staircase, his thoughts continued to revolve around her. Why was it that this young woman seemed to touch off some chord of memory within him? When Letty had told him Jane Tarrant's history, too, he had felt as though he must have heard it before. Yet to his knowledge he had never set eyes on her before that day in the Library.

His brows came down in a frown. It was uncanny—almost as uncanny as the fact that he could not remember what had happened to him in Kent, or how he had come to be back again in London. Nor was this all that troubled him; of late, his sleep had been interrupted by dreams—or rather, by one recurrent dream. It was pointless and inconclusive, as dreams often are, but it never varied. He would dream that he was sitting in a cold and cheerless room, furnished very like a coffee-room of a small hostelry: the light in the room was pale and grey, like the ashes in the grate, and a shadow hovered near the window. He would stand up and walk towards this shadow, and then he would realise that it was the figure of a woman, staring from the window out into the road beyond. He never reached her side, for he would awake then, with a deep sense of loss.

He shrugged his broad shoulders angrily as he stepped into Celia's dainty boudoir. He was dimly conscious of her dismissing the abigail, and greeting him with a nice blend of conspiracy and tenderness. Damn Celia, he thought suddenly; why had he been such a fool as to embroil himself in her sordid affairs? His action had been quixotic in the extreme, and he deserved all he had got.

"Well, Richard?"

Celia spoke sharply. It was the second time she had uttered the words since he had entered the room.

He started, seeming to return from a long distance.

"I beg your pardon. I was not attending."

"That is evident. I said, did you recover the letter?"

He looked at her eager face, then slowly shook his head.

"No."

The brightness faded from her glance, and was replaced by disappointment. She sank wearily into a chair.

"Did you try Julian?"

"Yes."

He was more alert now; the impressions of the last few minutes had left him. He walked over to the fire, and stood with his back to it, looking down into her face, which was moody and petulant.

"I broke into his house, and searched among his papers. My God, Celia, nothing but bills, I assure you! However, I expect you know how it is with him. He came downstairs, unluckily, and discovered me at the business."

She sat up, intent.

"He did? Then what happened?"

"We had a heart to heart talk," said Richard, with a dry smile. "He denied any knowledge of the whereabouts of the letter. Of course, he would. I realise; nevertheless, he managed to convince me. I don't think he has it."

"I told you he had not," snapped Celia. "Now what are we to do?"

She rose, clasping her hands to her head in a frenzy of despair.

"While that letter is at large, I cannot know an easy moment!"

"What exactly was in it?" asked Richard, curiously. He appeared unmoved by her performance.

She stared at him, incredulously.

"Do you mean to say that you didn't read it when you had the opportunity?"

"Can you seriously suppose I would?" he asked, amazed.

She shrugged. "Why ever not? I, for one, should not have blamed you. Curiosity is natural enough."

"If we were to be guided only by what is natural—however, this is no time for a discussion of ethics. Was there anything in that letter which could lead a chance reader to you? A name, for instance?"

"Oh, it was the usual kind of thing," she said, shrugging again. "No, I don't think there was any clear indication—I signed it with my initial, and referred to Francis by his; no more."

He began to pace about the room, deep in thought. After a moment, he wheeled round upon her.

"Then there seems no reason why it should ever find its way into Bordesley's hand—assuming, of course, that it was stolen by any ordinary thief."

"Oh, Richard!"

The significant tone of his last remark had quite escaped her. Relief flooded over her, and she ran to him in ecstasy, throwing her arms impetuously about him. With a man's blind instinct, he gathered her close. A pulse began to beat in his temples as the cloying perfume which she used wafted up to him. She raised her head, her deep blue eyes compelling his. She was fickle, he thought desperately, and heartless; cold, calculating, artificial—but desirable, by God, eminently desirable . . .

His eyes fixed themselves upon her soft red lips: they were drawing him irresistibly.

A shadow passed suddenly between him and the woman whom he held in his arms, the dark shadow of an unknown girl in a cold room at daybreak. The moment of temptation passed. With a quick gesture, he disengaged himself, and returned to his stance by the hearth.

With difficulty Celia contained her chagrin. This was a new Richard, indeed. What then? The greater sport to captivate him.

"There is one contingency, however," he said, as though nothing had interrupted his first speech, "which we would do well to take into account."

A quick frown creased her brows. "I don't understand. You said—"

"I said assuming that the thief was any ordinary felon. But my conversation with Summers revealed another possibility. It seems that his valet has been missing ever since my visit to Farrowdene. It occurred to us both that he might be the guilty party."

"Julian's man—what's his name?—Perkins?" asked Celia, in amazement. "But why on earth should he turn to robbery and violence? Servants do steal, of course, a little here and there, as everybody knows, but to attack a gentleman and rob him, giving up a good situation for the sake of a few paltry trinkets and a purse which may be light, for all he could know—no, I don't believe it possible!"

"There is a great deal in what you say. But Summers threw more light on the matter. It seems that this fellow is enamoured of your abigail, Betty. Summers suggested that they might have been acting in collusion. If by any chance Betty overheard our previous conversation in this room—"

Celia's face became a mask of fury. She clenched her hands until the nails bit into her flesh.

"So that's it!" she said, in a harsh, grating tone. "Yes, I can well believe that! The bitch! the dirty, impudent slut! Just wait until I get my hands on her!"

Sir Richard caught her arm quickly as she turned to the bedchamber: the bell-rope there rang straight through into the abigail's room.

"Wait! You must handle her gently, Celia."

"I am very likely to do that!"

"You will be foolish to do otherwise. Remember that we do not know for certain that she is concerned in this. Moreover—" as Celia opened her lips to interrupt him "—even if she is, there are things we can discover only from her. Speak her fair—try and find out where this fellow is now—say you are prepared to buy the letter from him, if necessary."

She checked in her swift rush to the bedchamber, and stood for a moment or two, turning over in her mind what he had said.

"Yes, I believe you are right," she admitted grudgingly. "Very well, then, we will handle Mistress Betty gently."

Contrary to her custom, tonight Celia had dismissed the girl to her bed. Dearly as Betty would have liked to eavesdrop on her mistress and Sir Richard, she had not dared to linger in the vicinity of the boudoir. The bell disturbed her, therefore, in the act of disrobing. She quickly flung on again the garments she had discarded, and hurried down the stairs which led from her attic chamber.

My lady was all sweetness.

"Come in, Betty," she began, with a disarming smile. "There are one or two questions I should like to put to you."

A wary expression came into the girl's eyes.

"Yes, m'lady?"

"I believe you are acquainted with Perkins, Mr. Summers' man?" asked Celia, watching her narrowly.

The girl's colour changed, and her expression became more guarded than before.

"I—I am a little, m'lady."

Celia raised her brows.

"A little? And yet I understood you to say, some months back, that you intended to wed the man."

"A girl may change her mind," replied Betty pertly, with a toss of her head.

"I'll change your mind for you, miss!" threatened Celia, advancing on her.

Betty backed hastily, and Sir Richard flung Celia a warning glance. She abandoned her antagonistic pose in response to this appeal, and a strained smile curved her lips.

"Come, we are old friends, Betty," she said, coaxingly. "We have no need of secrets from each other. Perkins has disappeared from Mr. Summers' house, and Sir Richard and I thought that you might possibly know where he can be found."

Betty made no answer to this, but looked warily from one to the other.

"I will be plain with you," continued Celia, in a confidential tone. "We believe that Perkins has something of great value to us. We would pay well to recover it."

Still Betty eyed them, uncertain what to say.

"If the—the article—could be recovered, we would not ask too many questions concerning its disappearance," went on Celia, persuasively.

"Perhaps I could help you more, m'lady, if I knew what it was you'd lost," ventured Betty, at last.

"A matter of a wallet, some gold fobs and seals, a watch, and a valuable jewelled snuff box," interposed Sir Richard at this point.

Betty started, surprised out of her caution.

"A jewelled snuff box? He never mentioned—"

To late she realised that she had betrayed herself: her hand came up to her mouth in dismay.

"So you do know all about it!" exclaimed Celia, seizing the girl and beginning to shake her. "Where is my letter, then, you baggage! Slut! So you listen at doors, do you, you trollop! I'll teach you if that shall pay!"

Thereupon, she launched a violent attack upon the abigail, hitting her about the face and ears, pouring forth at the same time such a vitriolic stream of abuse as almost brought the colour to Sir Richard's cheek.

"Here, I say, Celia!"

He moved forward to interfere as he saw the blood starting from the unfortunate abigail's nose. His intervention came too late, however, for at the same moment, the girl sank to the floor in a swoon.

Celia turned impatiently from her.

"You hear what she says, Richard? She must know where the letter is! Make her speak!"

She prodded the inanimate form forcibly with her foot. Sir Richard frowned heavily.

"Control yourself, Celia! You must bring her round before she can tell you anything more."

"I'd like to empty a pail of water over the creature, but for the ruining of my good carpet!" stormed Celia. "Betty, hi, Betty! You'd best come to, you hussy, or I'll find a way to bring you to your senses! She's shamming, Richard, I declare!"

"Nonsense!" he said, curtly, bending over the senseless abigail. "Her malady is real enough. You'd best bathe that nose if you're anxious concerning your carpet; and perhaps a vinaigrette might serve to bring the girl round."

"I bathe the creature's nose!" exclaimed Celia, in disgust. "I would as soon tend a rattlesnake! But she must and shall tell us more! I'll fetch Jane Tarrant, that's it! She will know what is to be done!"

So saying, she ran from the room, and began pounding upon the door of Jane's bedchamber.

Alarmed at the outcry, Jane came out quickly. "In Heaven's name, Celia, what is it?"

"It's Betty—my abigail—she's swooned away in my room—Jane, you must come and revive her instantly—instantly!"

She seized Jane by the arm and hustled her into the boudoir.

Jane stood still for a moment, taking in the scene. The abigail lay prostrate by the sofa, the blood from her nose staining her face and neck and the frilly white collar of her gown. Beside her stood Sir Richard Carisbrooke, in the helpless attitude of all males faced with a female crisis.

"Well, do you mean to stand there all night?" Celia asked Jane sharply. "Do something, pray!"

Jane roused herself, and set about tending the abigail. The others watched, Celia impatiently, while she fetched a basin of water, and began gently to cleanse Betty's face. When this was done, she raised the girl's head, holding a smelling-bottle under her nose. After a few moments, Betty stirred, and gave a convulsive shudder. Celia let out an exclamation of triumph.

They were all so intent upon the business in hand, that

they failed to hear the door open softly behind them. The sound of a voice made them turn sharply in that direction.

"Dear me, there appears to be a slight contretemps!" it drawled.

CHAPTER XV

THE INGENUITY OF MY LADY

AT THE SOUND of her husband's voice, my lady's expression changed to one of alarm. She cast an unguarded glance at Sir Richard. It was not lost upon the Earl.

"You appear to lead a most exciting life in my absence, my love," he said, smoothly. "I am delighted to feel you so well entertained. Er—your servant, Carisbrooke."

Sir Richard returned the salutation as coolly as he might. The situation was fraught with difficulty.

Betty chose this moment to revive fully, and sitting upright, immediately burst into a flood of tears.

"Hold your tongue, creature!" snapped Celia. She was momentarily at a loss. The Earl's appearance had for the time being put an end to all possibility of questioning the abigail further, and placed herself and Sir Richard in a very awkward predicament.

"You appear to be in some disorder, girl," said the Earl, not unkindly, taking in the details of Betty's swollen nose and blood-stained collar. "You'd best get you to bed."

Betty leapt up with alacrity, and, holding her apron to her face, ran from the room, thankful to escape. Jane made as if to follow her.

"One moment," said the Earl, detaining her by a gesture. "I desire you to remain, Miss Tarrant, if you please."

He turned indolently to Celia, who was standing uncertainly in the middle of the room, her mind racing furiously.

"I think you will agree, my dear, that I am entitled to some explanation of this extraordinary scene," he said drily, drawing forth a snuff box from his pocket, and inhaling a pinch.

His eyes travelled slowly round the group as he returned the box to his pocket in leisurely fashion, then flicked an imaginary speck of dust from his sleeve with a lace-bordered kerchief.

A moment passed, in which the ticking of the clock could be clearly heard. No one moved or spoke. Then Sir Richard started forward.

"I can explain, my lord," he began. "If you will have the goodness to hear me in private—"

There was nothing for it but to attempt to take the blame of this clandestine meeting upon himself, shielding Celia as best he might. It would be difficult enough, he reflected ruefully as he spoke. Invention was not his strong suit; he could have wished for a little more time in which to concoct a story that would leave the lady blameless.

But he had reckoned without Celia herself. She was in no need of any assistance in inventing a plausible tale. She broke in upon him now, a look of ineffable sweetness on her face.

"No, Sir Richard, I will tell him."

She was once more poised and collected; gone was all trace of the woman who had stormed and ranted like any fishwife barely ten minutes since. She turned to Jane, who was an embarrassed spectator of the scene.

"I do not think you can any longer hope to keep your secret, dearest Jane. Forgive me if I betray your confidence, but I imagine that Sir Richard himself was about to do so."

Jane stared in amazement.

"I?" she gasped. "I cannot—"

"Do not be alarmed," cut in Celia, swiftly. "After all, there is no reason why my husband should be angry with you. Francis—" she turned to the Earl, who was watching all the actors in this comedy with a faint amusement in his green eyes "—you must not be vexed with Jane. She has acted most nobly throughout the whole of this unhappy affair, as I told her when she took me into her confidence. Indeed, I know you will not blame her!"

The Earl bowed.

"Your dependence on my charity is infinitely flattering, my love. Nevertheless, before I can undertake to forgive Miss Tarrant, I must first know what transgression she has committed."

"As to that," said Celia, glibly, "it is not so very great a fault. Only consider her situation, with no connections, no fortune—and he in so very different a case!"

"I promise to consider all these things," drawled the Earl. "Perhaps you will come to the point, my life."

Celia clasped her hands together in an attitude of supplication.

"Could anything be more romantic? You must see it in that light, Francis, I know! Jane and Sir Richard Carisbrooke have entered into a secret engagement!"

This announcement was not without effect upon her hearers. The Earl raised his brows, and smiled. Jane started, and turned pale. Sir Richard took a hasty step forward.

"Hell and the devil, Celia—!"

"You make very free with my wife's name, sir," said the Earl, drily.

"I beg your pardon—this is not a time when I can choose my words—I—"

"Sir Richard," cut in Celia, glibly, "has been through a trying time, you must admit, Francis. To be enamoured of a lady, and forced to abjure her company—oh, my lord, you must see the tragedy of it!"

Amusement deepened in the Earl's eyes.

"Must I?" he murmured.

He moved to a chair.

"I beg you will all be seated. I am curious to know more of this—er—touching romance."

For a moment, Sir Richard's eyes, dark with annoyance and concern, met Jane's across the room. He frowned, puzzled; surely the girl's held pain in their grey depths? He silently heaped curses upon Celia's head. How like her to ease herself out of a scrape by putting others into one! What did it matter to her that this gentle creature who was, in a sense, in her power, might be turned out of doors without a character? He watched Jane while she made her way to the nearest chair in a daze.

"Well?" queried the Earl, after a pause. "You are all of you extremely reticent. Who is to begin the sad tale?"

"I think," began Sir Richard, grimly, "that my lady Bordesly would best do justice to it."

"I am perfectly of your opinion, my dear fellow," answered my lord, with a flash in his green eyes. "Celia, my love, I am waiting."

My lady made an endeavour to play for time.

"How is it that you are home tonight?" she parried. "I feared you would be obliged to be much longer absent."

"That is apparent. My affairs detained me less time than I had thought, and did not, in the event, take me so far from home. But do not let us postpone your interesting recital for such commonplaces. I am all attention."

Celia saw that there was no way out; the Earl meant to

hear this story, denying her the opportunity of time to improve upon it. She must simply do her best.

"Well, you see, Francis, it was this way. You may remember I told you that dearest Jane and I were at school together?"

The Earl nodded, for the first time fixing his eyes upon his wife's companion. A faint frown creased his brows.

"Sir Richard's sister was also a pupil in Miss Leasowe's establishment: she and Jane were the greatest of friends. That is how Jane first met Sir Richard."

"What is?" asked the Earl.

Celia stared at him for a moment, trying to pierce his mask. Was he really deceived by this farrago of hers, she wondered? Surely he must be, or else why did he appear to be so much amused? He had never before smiled when he had suspected her of a clandestine meeting with another man; and this meeting in her own room was so very much more damning than the encounter with Julian at the theatre, which had led to such a violently jealous scene afterwards. There was no help for it, she must plunge onwards with her story, and hope for the best.

"Why, I mean of course, that Sir Richard and Jane constantly encountered each other, as she and Letty were such friends."

"I take it, then, that Miss Tarrant visited at her friend's home?" asked the Earl.

"Oh, naturally!" replied Celia, hurriedly.

"I thought we had better make that clear," drawled my lord. "Otherwise it is difficult to imagine that there could have been many meetings between a young lady at a Seminary in Kensington, and a man up at Oxford. Continue, my love."

Sir Richard choked, and hastily covered the sound with a cough. The Earl was a cool hand, and no mistake! He began to feel that the fellow was wasted on Celia.

"Well, that is almost all there is to tell," went on Celia, a little annoyed by her husband's attitude. "They fell in love, and R— I mean, Sir Richard—begged Jane to marry him. But her father had been killed in action, she was in reduced circumstances, and felt that it was unfair to him to agree."

"That is just what I should suppose of her," said the Earl; and for once his tone was completely serious.

Sir Richard frowned. There was a hint of warmth in the Earl's manner; for some obscure reason, he found himself resenting it. Celia, too, noticed the change. Well, if Francis had any fancy towards Jane, as she had often suspected, this story must put an end to his hopes. She smiled, triumphant in the knowledge that she was killing two birds with one stone.

"Sir Richard was not so easily put off," she continued. "At last he succeeded in prevailing upon her to enter into a secret engagement."

"And the date of this engagement, my life?" purred the Earl.

Celia paused.

"Oh, I am not perfectly certain—is it two or three years since, Jane?"

Jane looked up, alarmed at being applied to, and murmured something unintelligible. She felt utterly wretched. It was the cruellest irony that Celia, in her desire to extricate herself from a tight corner, should have chanced upon this particular subterfuge. Was it indeed chance, or did she suspect the truth? Certainly she had guessed that Jane cherished a secret love, but was she yet aware of the object of that passion?

It made no difference, thought Jane despairingly. The harm was done, and, for the life of her, Jane could see no way out of it. She could not give the lie to Celia without betraying not only her but Sir Richard. Her mind flinched from such an act, from its probable consequences—a scandal, a duel, someone killed; perhaps the man she loved.

A slight smile curved my lady's lips as her eyes rested on Jane. It was as though she could read the other's thoughts. Jane Tarrant would not betray her; such a course was utterly foreign to the girl's nature. And there was nothing to be feared from Richard ...

The Earl, too, was remembering what his wife had said concerning Miss Tarrant's talent for helping others out of scrapes. His expression remained as inscrutable as ever.

"Then I am to infer, my love, that these two star-crossed lovers, knowing your tender heart, confided in you? And that you promoted their meeting secretly in your room?"

Once again, Celia was at a loss. She had quite decided that Francis could not possibly suspect the truth, or else his behaviour would have been very different. But how else to account for his strange manner?

"Yes, that was the way of it," she answered reluctantly.

"But it is charming, my dear!"

The Earl spread his arms in an expansive gesture.

"And so like you!"

Now Celia was really alarmed: Francis was acting most oddly. Sir Richard, too, watched the Earl curiously. Only Jane seemed too deep in her own thoughts to notice anything amiss.

"I congratulate you, Carisbrooke," said the Earl suddenly. "You have gained more than you deserve."

"Why, so I think!" answered Sir Richard, spontaneously.

"You must beware, my dear fellow," drawled the Earl, with the first hint of steel in his voice. "The luck cannot favour you all the time."

Sir Richard bowed, and Celia glanced sharply at her husband. But the Earl was watching Jane with compassion in his eyes.

"We must talk of this again," he said, with a delicately smothered yawn. "I have found it utterly fascinating. However, the hour is well advanced, and I see that Miss Tarrant is weary. You will not think us inhospitable, I trust, Carisbrooke, if we defer our raptures to another time? I have had a long journey, and had thought to spend a quiet evening at home. You will allow me to escort you downstairs."

Sir Richard could not but feel thankful to have the scene thus brought to a close. He bowed distantly to my lady, hesitated a second, then took a step forward in the direction of Jane's chair. She looked up at his approach; he winced at the pain in her eyes.

"Miss Tarrant!" he said, impetuously. "I ask your pardon—indeed, I am sorry—"

She gave no sign, but remained staring vacantly before her, as though there had been no one else in the room.

"I await your pleasure, my dear Carisbrooke," drawled the Earl, ever watchful.

Sir Richard started, sketched a hasty bow, and turned on his heel to follow the other man from the room.

CHAPTER XVI

A FUGITIVE

SIR RICHARD slowly descended the steps leading into the Square, confused thoughts chasing round his mind. He tried to put them straight: Bordesley, for instance, what exactly was he up to? Only a fool could have believed him to be deceived by Celia's tale; and yet, if he was not, why had he appeared to be so amused? His reputation as a jealous husband was notorious, and the secretive way in which Celia had conducted this whole affair bore out the rumours. Yet undoubtedly he had been amused by Celia's recital. Was it because be believed Sir Richard to have been playing a double game with my lady? That argued that he credited the engagement.

Sir Richard grimaced; he did not care to appear in the light of a gay deceiver to anyone. It was possible, however, that Bordesley had made a show of accepting the story for the benefit of the ladies. Later, the inevitable challenge would follow. Well, that did not worry him, though he would have preferred his opponent to be five and twenty years younger. He had no taste for meeting a man old enough to be his father. Bordesley was a rattling good shot, however; in that sense, they would be evenly matched.

That young woman, Celia's companion—what the devil was to be done about her? Even if Bordesley did find the whole business amusing, he might well take a very strong line about harbouring a female who indulged in secret meetings with men in his house. He would very likely turn her off without a character, and then—

He had lingered at the foot of the steps, and now turned to quit the Square, impatiently thrusting away his thoughts. As he did so, he all but cannoned into a flying, dark-cloaked figure which suddenly ran up the area steps and into the street. Instinctively he made a grab for the fugitive.

"Here, hold on!" He tightened his grasp. "Where are you off to in such a devil of a hurry—who are you, anyway?"

123

The figure let out a sob.

"Let me go, please, Sir Richard! Let me go!"

He looked down quickly at the sound of the voice, and thrust back the hood of the cloak.

"Why, 'pon rep, it's Betty!"

"Yes, y'r honour—let go of me—please do—I've got to get away!"

The abigail struggled violently, but could not shake off the man's firm clasp.

"No, be damned if you do!" he said, quickly. "You're going to tell me all about Perkins first!"

"I daresn't—oh, please do let me go, you—you're hurting me!"

"It won't hurt if you don't struggle," said Sir Richard, practically. "But you're quite wrong about Perkins, my girl; what you don't seem to realise is that you daren't keep silent. For if you don't tell me the whole instantly, I mean to call up the Watch, and give you in charge for conniving at theft and assault."

The abigail stopped struggling, and looked up at him. By the pale light of the moon, the man saw the horror in her face.

"Oh, no!"

"Oh, yes!" mocked Sir Richard, grimly. "I am determined to get to the bottom of this affair."

"Then let's get away from here first, y'r honour, if you please! I've no wish to be discovered—for go back I never will, and so I swear! I can't put up with my lady's ways any longer—I hope she—"

"That will do!" interrupted Sir Richard, although he could not help feeling a certain sympathy for the girl. She had caused him trouble enough, but he felt that Celia's attack on her had done much to cancel out the debt he owed her for that.

"I have no interest in hearing your views on your mistress; what concerns me is this other matter. We will walk on a little, and you can tell me all you know."

He released her arm cautiously, prepared to make another grab at her if she should try to escape him. But she evidently realised the uselessness of such a course, for she fell into step beside him, clutching more firmly the bundle which she carried. She turned a pleading face towards him.

"If I can get back the things you've lost, y'r honour, will

you let me go, and promise not to set the law on Perkins?"
she begged breathlessly.

He looked at her sternly.

"You're in no position for bargaining. Come, I want to
hear how all this started. Were you listening at the keyhole
when first I visited your mistress?"

"Such as me have to make their way as best they can,"
whined Betty.

"So you did listen? What did you hear?"

She shot him a crafty glance, and did not answer. He
seized her ungently by the arm.

"Out with it! I'm determined to know; so be quick about
it. If you take too long, we'll see if a Bow Street Runner can
loosen your tongue for you."

It would be difficult to say whether the threat of the Law,
or the pressure of the strong hand on her arm worked more
powerfully on Betty. However it was, she abandoned all attempt at bargaining or evasion: bit by bit, Sir Richard ex-
tracted the story from her.

It seemed that when Betty heard of the existence of an indiscreet letter of my lady's, which was to be found in the
possession of Mr. Summers, she had immediately sent a note
to Perkins by way of a cousin of hers who was a carrier. She
had instructed Perkins to try and find the letter before Sir
Richard should arrive in Kent with the money that had been
asked as its price. Perkins had dutifully hunted amongst his
master's effects, but the most painstaking search had failed to
bring the document to hand before Sir Richard's arrival at
Farrowdene. Desperate, and unable to consult with Betty,
who was the brains of the partnership, the valet had formu-
lated a plan on the spur of the moment.

This was to ride ahead a mile or so on the road which he
knew Sir Richard would follow back to London. Betty
glossed over the next part of the plan, which had been to
waylay Sir Richard and force him to hand over the letter at
the point of a pistol. She laid great stress on the fact that
Perkins had not expected Sir Richard to put up any resist-
ance, and that the blow on the head which had followed had
been entirely fortuitous.

"He told me he was fair demented when he saw you lying
senseless there on the ground, not knowing for sure how
badly you was hurt," continued Betty. "He started to turn everything out of your pockets to look for the letter; but he
was so on edge, what with you looking like one dead, and

him fearing that at any minute someone might pass that way, that he didn't make no great headway with the search. In the end, he decided to take all the things along with him, and look through them properly later, when he'd got away from that place."

"So he went, leaving me to my fate," said Sir Richard, grimly. "An attractive character, your Perkins! He richly deserves the hanging I feel sure will one day overtake him. And what did he do with my poor mare, pray? She must have been frightened out of her wits."

"He left her at a nearby inn," answered the girl, "saying that his master would call for her in a day to two. Your honour needn't worry over the horse—she'll be there safe enough yet."

"Where is this place?"

She hesitated.

"I don't rightly know, y'r honour."

"Then lead me to this fellow Perkins," ordered Sir Richard, peremptorily. "I mean to clear up this affair, once for all."

The abigail clutched at his arm.

"Oh, no, indeed I can't, Sir Richard—I promised not to tell anyone where he is—"

"Honour among thieves, eh?"

He reflected rapidly for a moment. No doubt he was a fool, but he did not care to bully the abigail into betraying her man. Who knows, perhaps the girl was genuinely in love with him: she seemed to be a mean, crafty piece of goods, but appearances could be deceptive.

"I'll tell you what," he said abruptly. "If I can recover my property and my horse, I'm prepared to forget about the assault on my person. You take me to this fellow, and I'll guarantee that if he hands the things over intact, I'll leave it at that."

It was some time before he could persuade Betty that he meant what he said. At last, however, he did succeed in convincing her, and she confided to him that Perkins had taken refuge with a relative of his who owned a small tavern in the City. Sir Richard was determined to set off there at once, but, after some argument, the abigail managed to dissuade him from this course. She said that Perkins would be abed long since, and the place shut up for the night. Sir Richard's arrival in the small hours would create the kind of stir that might well bring the Watch down upon them.

This suggestion gave him pause: he felt that he had enjoyed more than enough excitement for one evening.

"You can come there tomorrow, y'r honour, and talk to him as private as may be in a room at the back of the tap. I'll go there first thing in the morning, and prepare him for your coming. My cousin the carrier's wife'll give me a bed for the night, I hope—what's left of it."

"An excellent arrangement," approved Sir Richard. "And now you may give me the bundle you're carrying."

She looked startled, and asked why.

"You cannot suppose that I am such a mutton-head as to trust you without any surety for your good behaviour?" he asked scornfully. "I dare say there are things in this bundle you would not lose for any money, otherwise you wouldn't have stayed to put them together in a moment of such urgency. I will be at this place tomorrow at—"

He paused, considering. "At mid-day," he resumed. "If I don't find your friend there, I go at once to Bow St., and acquaint them with the whole. If he should be there, however, and should answer my questions satisfactorily, I will leave your bundle with him—unless you mean to be present yourself."

Betty was obliged to concur in this plan, and to hand over her bundle; which she did very reluctantly, for, as he had guessed, it contained more than one valuable trinket given her by my lady, and some few which she had quietly abstracted from the jewel case, secure in the knowledge that they would never be missed, as they were pieces of which her mistress had grown tired. What Betty could manage to raise on these would prove the basis of her future existence, for she would find it difficult to obtain another post as lady's maid, having quitted her present one without the benefit of a character.

Indeed, although she would not positively starve, her prospects did not look nearly so rosy as on that night when she had listened at the door of my lady Bordesley's boudoir, and thought gleefully that at last she had found the way to easy riches.

She parted from Sir Richard almost persuaded that honesty was the best policy, a maxim which she had been made to write out many times at the little Dame school which she had attended in her childhood, but which had somehow until now never held for her the ring of truth.

Sir Richard took his way homewards, bundle under his

arm, deep in thought. His reflections, however, were centered not on the interview which he had arranged for twelve o'clock the next day, but upon one which he planned to attend at an earlier hour in the morning.

CHAPTER XVII

A PROPOSAL OF MARRIAGE

"There's a lady downstairs asking to see you, ma'am."

Jane turned her head towards the maid lingering in the doorway.

"A lady calling? And for me, Molly?"

The surprise in her tone was justified. It was a little after nine o'clock in the morning, much too early for social calls. Moreover, who should call on Miss Tarrant?

"Yes, ma'am. It's a Miss Carisbrooke, if you please. Will you see her, ma'am? Baker put her in the hall, not being sure—"

"Yes, of course; thank you, Molly. I will see Miss Carisbrooke in the morning-room."

The maid bobbed and shut the door. Jane paused a moment or two in wonder before following her downstairs.

Letty? What could her friend want with her at this time of day? She had said, too, that she would never call here for fear of encountering Celia; why this sudden change? Could she possibly have heard anything of the doings of yesterday evening—but no: Sir Richard would not speak to his sister of his assignations with his mistress.

Completely mystified, Jane made her way slowly to the morning-room. Letty looked up expectantly as she entered, and sprang to her feet.

"Dearest Jane, you must tell me what all the mystery is! Here am I come round on an errand to you from Richard, and he is as close as any oyster as to its meaning! But you'll not be so cruel, will you, Jane? You both assured me that you did not know each other, and now Riccy has sent me to beg that you will grant him an interview—as though one holds interviews with people one doesn't know! It is all to do with that horrid Celia, I feel persuaded, and if you don't mean to tell me, Jane, I declare it will be the shabbiest trick!"

129

She paused for breath.

"Your brother desired you to ask me for an interview?" asked Jane, changing colour.

Letty eyed her suspiciously.

"Upon my word, you are both behaving very strangely! I do not know what to think! Can it be—?"

"What exactly did Sir Richard say?" interrupted Jane, afraid of what her friend might be about to ask.

"He said that it was imperative for him to see you at once, but that he had no wish to seek you out here, for reasons which he seemed to think you must know. He therefore asked me to beg that you would accompany me in the carriage back to our house, so that he might have an opportunity of talking with you uninterrupted."

"I see."

Jane walked restlessly about the room for a while in silence. An interview with Sir Richard was one of the last things she desired, afraid as she was of betraying her feelings; yet it was necessary that they should see each other to decide what was to be done concerning Celia's wild story of their secret engagement. It was only reasonable, she told herself, that he should wish to discuss the matter with her, and she well understood that he would not want to come here. Before he again encountered the Earl, he would have to be quite clear as to what was to be said to him: Jane herself had spent a sleepless night trying to work out that problem.

"Very well, Letty, I will come with you now. Only wait while I fetch my bonnet; I shall not be a moment."

She was as good as her word, returning in well under the time that her friend had expected. They left the house without more ado, Jane pausing an instant at the door to leave a message with the porter for Celia, who was not yet astir.

Letty managed to keep silence until they were settled in the carriage, and the horses urged forward into a trot; then she turned to Jane impetuously, and took her hands.

"Dear Jane, do tell me what is amiss, I pray, for you and Richard both look so miserable, there is no bearing it! I dare swear that wretched Celia has done something to make you both so unhappy; and if so, I beg you will not heed it, for very likely it is all a piece of malice. Oh, if only either of you would tell me anything, but you are both so discreet, there is no way of helping you! And I would do anything to help, as you must know, Jane, and so does Richard, only he feels that he cannot trust me!"

This speech could not but add to Jane's discomfiture. She longed to confide in her friend, but how was it to be done? It was not to be supposed that Letty, chatterbox as she was, could refrain from dropping a hint or two to her brother, if she knew Jane's story. To be possessed of a secret, and to live in the same house as the one person, who, of all others, must remain in ignorance of it—that was asking too much of human nature in general, and particularly of Letty Carisbrooke.

"I beg you not to importune me for an answer," said Jane, returning the pressure of Letty's hand. "Believe me, if only I were at liberty to speak, there is no one in whom I would more gladly confide; you must know that. But I can't tell you anything without revealing matters which are not mine to divulge."

Letty sighed, and withdrew her hands from Jane's clasp.

"I suppose I must believe you, but it is very tiresome to know that something is going on, and not be able to draw a word out of anyone to the purpose! Oh, dear, here we are! I do wish I knew what all this means!"

There was no time for more to be said on either side, for the door of the carriage was opened by the servants, and the two young ladies passed into the house.

Letty guided her friend into a small salon on the ground floor, tastefully furnished in red and gold.

"It is too early for Mama," she apologised, "so I am sorry that she cannot receive you. Perhaps after you have talked with Richard—"

Here she was interrupted, for the door opened, and Sir Richard came into the room. Jane's heart missed a beat as she glanced up and saw him; she thought how strong and dependable he looked, with his broad shoulders and firm chin. It was impossible to believe that he could play a dishonourable part; yet surely there could be no doubt of it?

He bowed formally, and to her dismay Jane felt the colour rising to her cheeks. Her eyes dropped away from his.

Letty surveyed Jane's flushed face and her brother's somewhat stern air, which she knew to be due to embarrassment, with a perplexed glance.

"Well, I expect you will like to be private," she said, with a sigh of resignation. "You will not go without first seeing me, Jane?"

Jane promised something, hardly knowing what she said, and Letty quitted the room, leaving them alone.

After she had gone, there was a long silence. The man did not sit, but stood leaning one arm on the chimneypiece, as though seeking support. At length, he spoke.

"We find ourselves in a very awkward situation, Miss Tarrant."

Jane breathed an assent, without raising her eyes. He studied her for a moment, then quickly looked away again.

"The question is, what is to be done or said?"

It was a question to which she had found no answer through a long night. She said nothing.

"We cannot deny the story," he went on, with a frown, "although God knows Celia deserves little enough loyalty from either of us."

Jane looked up at this.

"I am surprised that you should say so, sir," she said, with biting emphasis.

He stared, obviously at a loss.

"I? I suppose it is ungallant in me."

"It is conduct," said Jane, spiritedly, "that is unworthy of any man in your situation!"

He turned round to face her squarely, and saw the indignation in her grey eyes.

"Why, what's this?" he asked abruptly; then a flash of illumination crossed his countenance.

"Yes, I see," he said, slowly.

He took a turn or two about the room before he spoke again. When he did, his eyes avoided hers.

"Perhaps I don't deserve that you should think so harshly of me, Miss Tarrant. It is true that once I was at Celia's feet—"

He broke off, faced with the impossibility of revealing to her any circumstances which might place his actions in a better light, or give her a different notion of his character. He saw that she had drawn the inevitable conclusion from his nocturnal visits to Celia, and for a moment, he longed desperately to set her right. He could not betray Celia's confidence, however, and what other way was there to convince this young lady? He shrugged his shoulders helplessly.

Jane had caught her breath at his last words; did he say that he was once at Celia's feet? But that must mean—yet why had he been meeting her in secret, if he no longer cared for her? There could be only one explanation for such conduct, an explanation which his slight shrug seemed to bear out. He was no longer in love with Celia, but meant still to enjoy her favours.

Her eyes flashed fire, but her voice was cold as ice.

"I do not think of you in any way at all, sir."

His brows came down in a heavy frown. He had known that this interview was going to be deuced difficult, but he had never imagined the half, he told himself grimly. Decidedly it was not proceeding on the lines he had planned. He determined to make a fresh start.

"Tell me, Miss Tarrant," he began, abruptly abandoning the preceding pointless topic, "did you feel that Bordesley was deceived by Celia's tale?"

She considered this for a moment, her indignation abating.

"I do not know; he seemed to be very amused, which argues that he did—and yet—"

"Exactly my impression! You must know, of course, his reputation as a jealous husband; had he believed that Celia was covering up—"

He paused, embarrassed: then continued quickly—"Had he not believed her story, he must have acted very differently. Yet one could not escape the feeling that he saw through the whole thing, and was baiting her."

Jane nodded her agreement.

"You did not see him before you came out?" he asked.

"No." She shook her head. "Neither he nor Lady Bordesley were astir."

"That is well," he said. "At least it gives us the opportunity to tell the same tale—for I don't doubt that Bordesley will question you further; and I must, in common civility, give him some account of my actions."

It was on the tip of Jane's tongue to say that, had he acted as he ought, there would be no need of any subterfuge. She was dismayed to find how much she wanted to say something that would hurt him. Even now, when all the evidence was against him, she could not really bring herself to believe that he was the kind of man to conduct a secret love affaire with another man's wife. This warring within herself of instinct and reason seemed to inflame her more strongly against him. Had she been able to convince herself of his perfidy, she thought, how easily would her love have turned to contempt!

She was silent for so long that he came over to a chair close to hers, and, seating himself, regarded her gravely for some minutes. At length, he broke the silence.

"Every time we meet, Miss Tarrant, I become more convinced that we have encountered each other somewhere before. Letty told me something of your history the other day, and I was struck then by the ring of familiarity which the story held for me. Is it possible that we have indeed met before you came here to Celia Bordesley?"

Jane hardly dared to speak. Should she tell him when and where they had met? She remembered his assignations with Celia; jealousy shook her. No, she would never, never seek to bring to his memory that which it seemed he had so easily forgotten! She knew in her heart that this was not fair, that his loss of memory was something for which he could not possibly be blamed, something far removed from careless forgetfulness; but she was once more tortured by strong feelings, and could not be rational in her attitude towards him.

"I suppose it is possible, sir."

Her answer surprised herself by its calm, casual tone: how easy it was, after all, to say words that were very different from her feelings.

He appeared disappointed. "But you have no recollection of it? Then it must be one of those strange affinities one reads of—though I must say such things are not much in my line in the general way!"

He paused, and went on again in a more businesslike tone.

"I've been wondering how all this will affect your future. Do you suppose that Bordesley will turn you off?"

Jane nodded calmly. "I have considered that possibility. I imagine he must: he's bound to feel that I have acted with a lack of propriety that is unsuitable in his wife's companion."

The dark brows drew together.

"What can I possibly say to you, Miss Tarrant? Between us, Celia and I have injured you irremediably!"

"Do not concern yourself," said Jane, quietly. "I had no intention of remaining in the Bordesley household any longer than was necessary. This business merely hurries on my plans. I shall pack up and leave instantly."

"But where will you go?"

"I have friends to whom I can go for a time, at least. My lawyer—"

"Your lawyer?" he repeated swiftly. "I—"

His voice tailed off, as a puzzled look came into his eyes. Jane waited, her heart in her mouth. Was it possible that this chance word of hers might remind him of the day when they had set off together to call upon that same lawyer?

A minute passed, during which neither spoke. Then the man seemed to collect himself.

"But—forgive me, I am obliged to say this—I understood from Letty that your financial position—"

He floundered unhappily, not wishing to embarrass her. She came to his rescue.

"I shall be obliged to find another post, of course. I should not dream of remaining with my friends for any length of time."

"But won't it be difficult?" he asked. "It is unlikely that Bordesley will give you a reference in the circumstances, I suppose."

"I have others," answered Jane with dignity.

"I am sure you have!" he said warmly. "And couched in the highest terms, I make no doubt! But if this unfortunate affair should leak out—and, in any case, Bordesley believes us to be engaged—or, at least, I think he does—"

"Engagements have been broken before now," said Jane.

"You mean to tell him that we have put an end to it?"

"My affairs," said Jane, a little stiffly, "are really no concern of my lord Bordesley. He may be my employer for the moment, but that does not give him the right to pry into my private life. However, if it should be necessary to say anything on this subject, I shall tell him that I see no possibility of any happiness resulting to either party from a continuance of the engagement."

His eyes met hers as though he were seeing her for the first time.

"I believe, you know, Miss Tarrant, that some women in your situation would not so act," he remarked, slowly.

"No? But surely it puts an end to the affair quite neatly? Or do you see a difficulty which has escaped my notice?"

He shook his head. "No. But it occurs to me that a woman such as Celia, in a like case, might turn this fictitious engagement to her advantage."

"What do you mean?" she asked, frowning.

"Does it not offer a way of escape from a life which cannot but be tedious to you?"

She started, and looked uncertainly at him. He found that he could not meet her eyes, and fell to studying the pattern of the carpet.

"No doubt I am putting this very badly, Miss Tarrant, but bear with me. You have been used by Celia—I suppose I must take a share of the blame, too—in such a way that you will be put to a great deal of inconvenience, and may even find it difficult to obtain another post. Your future has been jeopardised, and I have had a hand—if unwillingly—in the doing of it. It touches my honour, and I therefore feel compelled to hold you to our so-called engagement."

"What are you saying?" gasped Jane, turning quite pale.

He looked up, his eyes gentle.

"I am asking if you will do me the honour of marrying me."

Jane pressed her hands to her bosom; she could feel the wild beating of her heart. Her mind was in a turmoil, and she was quite incapable of making any answer. He saw this, and watched her in silence for what seemed to Jane an infinity. At last, she grew calmer, and the mists cleared from before her eyes. She found her voice.

"Your motives do you credit, sir. I regret that I must decline."

Surprise showed on his face.

"Will you not think it over? It is a solution of your present difficulties—"

"I have not been used," said Jane, with trembling lips, "to think of marriage as a solution of my difficulties."

His glance lingered on the tremulous mouth, on the small face framed by its bright hair. What dreams might not lie behind those soft grey eyes, he wondered? Dreams, perhaps, such as he had once known, before Celia had trampled them underfoot.

Was he violating this girl's vision of love by suggesting a marriage of convenience to her? It was only too probable.

"Forgive me if I ask a blunt question," he said; and the abruptness of his tone served as a cover to his feelings. "Is there—anyone else, Miss Tarrant?"

"No," answered Jane, quickly. That at least was true.

"Then will you not consider my offer?" he countered, quickly. "Lord knows I would not readily counsel a marriage of convenience to any female; and you are young and attractive, if you will allow me to say so, and must have visualised a more romantic match. But the circumstances in this case are so difficult, and marriage such an obvious solution for us both—"

"I cannot marry without better reason than expediency," said Jane, striving to give firmness to her tone.

He leaned forward in his chair until his face was only a

short distance away from hers, fixing her with a steady regard from his dark eyes.

"You mean you will not marry without love?"

She nodded, trying to avoid his glance.

"There have, I believe, been instances of love coming after marriage: provided, of course, that the partners began on a note of mutual respect and esteem. I have a feeling for you, Miss Tarrant—" he paused, and took her hand, suddenly grown cold, into his—"already somewhat warmer than that—a feeling which would not take long, I dare swear, to blossom into—"

He broke off, and she felt the quick leaping of his pulse as it rested against her fingers. Her head seemed on fire, and her bosom rose and fell with her unsteady breathing.

What he read into her silence, she could not know; but suddenly he dropped her hand, and leapt to his feet.

"But of course," he continued, bitterly, "you have no reason to hold me in the same esteem."

It was as though a veil had been torn from before her eyes. No, she had no reason to esteem him, for was he not Celia's lover, even while he was seeking her hand in marriage? Even though, added her heart, striving desperately to be fair, even though his reasons for asking her to marry him were of the most honourable. It was more than likely, she told herself bitterly, that he was saying all this as a salve to her pride; he considered that he was bound in honour to marry her, and sought to make her acceptance of him easier by pretending to more than he really felt.

With an effort, she forced herself to speak calmly.

"You mean all for the best, I know, and you must not think me ungrateful. But there are reasons which make such a solution of my difficulties distasteful to me. You must let me go my own way."

He bowed.

"Very well, madam, if that is your wish. You are resolved, then, to tell Bordesley that the engagement is at an end?"

She rose as if to go, smoothing the folds of her dress to avoid meeting his eyes.

"If it should be necessary to speak of my affairs to his lordship, that is what I shall say."

She walked towards the door in what she hoped was a resolute manner.

"I wish you good day, sir," she said, with a curtsey. "I believe your sister is waiting for me."

He returned her farewell absentmindedly, holding the door open until she had passed through into the hall, where Letty was waiting at the foot of the stairs.

When she had gone, he closed the door, and came back into the room to stand before the fire, lost in thoughts.

What had persuaded him to ask Jane Tarrant's hand in marriage? Such a course had not entered his head when he had sought the interview. There was something about this girl, something that drew him on; and yet she was no charmer in the sense that Celia was. Could there be anything in that romantic nonsense that was sometimes talked of two people having met and loved in another incarnation?

He smiled: absurd. Yet he knew some regret that Jane Tarrant had not, after all, accepted him.

CHAPTER XVIII

JANE RECEIVES ANOTHER DECLARATION

JANE STAYED with Letty only a few minutes. After one glance at her face, her friend did not press her to remain and meet Lady Carisbrooke. There was more here than she could understand, but this much she knew—both Jane Tarrant and her brother were unhappy. She attributed this in some way to Celia Bordesley as a matter of course, and, whatever other speculations she made, she did not tease Jane with them. She contented herself with expressing a wish that they might soon meet again, bade her dear Jane come to her if there was the least little thing she could do to help in any way, and saw her friend into the carriage.

Jane's heart reproached her as she watched the dimpled little face, so serious now for the moment, recede into the distance. Perhaps the hardest thing of all was not to be able to take Letty into her confidence.

She did not have long to reflect on this, however, for she was soon arrived back in Grosvenor Square. The porter greeted her with a message to attend my lady instantly in her boudoir. Jane paused only to remove her bonnet before knocking upon Celia's door.

"Oh thank heaven you are come!" exclaimed Celia, eagerly, drawing Jane into the room. "I feared that Francis might get his hooks into you before I had a chance to speak first with you!"

"I have not yet seen my lord," answered Jane, taking in Celia's flushed cheek and flustered air.

"Again I thank Heaven! Jane, I want to throw myself on your mercy!"

She uttered these words with all the fervour of one condemned to the stake. Jane looked upon her coldly.

"You had little enough mercy on me last night," she returned.

Celia seized her arm, looking up at her from blue eyes dark with pleading; the distress on her lovely face would

139

have moved a statue to compassion. Jane thought how beautiful she was, and how impossible it seemed that anyone, especially a man, could ever resist her. It was sad to reflect that one so lovely could be so false.

"You will not betray me, Jane? I will give you anything you ask—I have an ample allowance from Bordesley, and you shall not find me ungenerous—there is a set of rubies, Jane, which I bought myself, and have worn only once—you shall have them, you shall have anything you desire, if only you will promise to hold to the tale I told Francis last night! Richard I know I can depend upon, and you—you cannot have changed so much, Jane! You were ever one to help others out of scrapes! It is not so very difficult a thing to do, or distasteful, for there is no gainsaying the fact that Richard is a handsome man! And after a little time, you can say you have quarrelled, or make some other excuse for breaking the engagement off!"

The words spilled out one after another, tripping each other up in their haste; the graceful hands made gestures of supplication. Jane was seized by a feeling of revulsion.

"You think of everything, do you not? But I'll put you out of your agony, Celia: I have no intention of betraying you. There is no need to bribe me."

"Dearest Jane! I knew I might rely upon you!"

The supplication dropped away from her expression, and was replaced by a calculating look.

"But your answers must be convincing should Francis question you—and I think it only fair to warn you that he is almost certain to do so, and not a particularly easy person to gammon."

She broke off, frowning.

"I cannot feel perfectly satisfied that he altogether believed me last night."

Jane moved away from her, relieved that her pleading was at an end. It was obvious that there were no depths to which she would not sink to gain her own way.

"I—we—were talking of that matter earlier today," Jane said, haltingly. "Sir Richard Carisbrooke and I, that is to say. He sent Letty here to fetch me to their house."

Celia stared.

"So that is where you have been! I was afraid that you might have run away and left me to face it out alone. But what an odd thing for Richard to have done—although I suppose it is natural enough that you should meet to concoct some tale that will tally with mine. Yes, on second thoughts, it was very wise of Richard! He will, of course, feel obliged to wait on Francis with an apology for drawing me into the affair; and it is essential that his account should correspond with yours. What did he say to you?"

To Jane's annoyance, she found herself blushing. Celia looked at her sharply.

"Why, what—but, of course, that is just what he would do! He was ever quixotic! I am right in thinking that he asked you to marry him?"

Jane's heart sank as she heard Celia putting into words her own thoughts on Sir Richard's motive for the proposal of marriage which he had made her. Once more she had to acknowledge that, against all reason, she had hoped that partiality might have moved him as much as expediency.

There seemed no point in denying something which Celia would in all probability very soon learn from Sir Richard himself. She nodded in answer to the question.

"Upon my word!" said Celia, tartly. "This has all turned out very well for you, after all, Jane! You will have no need now of my rubies—Richard will buy you some of your own, and diamonds as well, no doubt! I dare swear you will find him all that is generous. You will have quite a handsome fortune, Jane—not to be compared with mine, of course, for the Bordeslys are vastly rich—but still, a very elegant competence, especially for a penniless girl! And you will be my lady Carisbrooke—to be sure, Richard is only a baronet, but still, it is something. 'Pon rep, I think you should thank me for putting you in the way of such a splendid match!"

"You cannot suppose," asked Jane, wonderingly, "that I mean to accept him?"

Celia's lips parted in surprise, and she gazed at Jane as though the other had taken leave of her senses.

"Not mean to accept him? What folly is this?"

"You really imagine," said Jane, with a scornful flash of her grey eyes, "that I would accept a man who offers for me because he feels compelled in honour to do so? You must have a pretty notion of my character!"

"Stuff!" replied Celia, contemptuously. "What has character to say to it, pray? Here you have the chance—and believe me, Jane, I doubt if you'll ever get such a good one again— to put an end to this drudging life of yours, and make a match that half the debutantes of Town would envy you; and all you have the wit to do, is to refuse it! It may show character, you poor fool, but it shows precious little sense!"

Jane sighed. "It is impossible for us ever to see eye to eye on this subject, Celia," she said wearily. "Let us drop it, I beg."

"But do you not see what you are about?" asked Celia, incredulously. She found it impossible to grasp that anyone could be so blind to her own material advantage.

"You have told me before this that you do not find your way of life tedious," she continued. "That may be true, though I for one cannot credit it; but only think how this marriage could change your circumstances! Do you suppose that anyone half as good a catch as Richard will ever come seeking you out? If you manage to lay hold of a curate or a tradesman, you may count yourself fortunate. And most likely you will never marry at all, but go on, becoming older and dowdier year by year, as you slave away at teaching those frightful brats: until in the end you are too old for the life, and must think yourself fortunate if you even have a roof over your head! What extraordinary reason can you have for such arrant folly?"

"I cannot face the prospect of a loveless marriage," answered Jane, her face pale. "Better, I think, the evils which you picture so dramatically."

"Love!" scoffed Celia. "Always this talk of love! Bah, it sickens me! Leave love to the menfolk, Jane; our business is to captivate, not to be captivated!"

"I must act as I feel right. I mean nothing to Sir Richard Carisbrooke. Tied to me for life, he might easily come to detest the very sight of me."

Something in her tone caught Celia's attention. She eyed Jane sharply.

"So that's it!" she exclaimed, triumphantly. "He is the man for whom you nourish this secret passion that has been puzzling me for so long!"

Jane covered her face with her hands, but too late; already it had betrayed her.

"Well!" said Celia, in tones of surprise. "But how has all this come about, pray? For I am tolerably sure that you never met Richard until you came to this house. But stay!"

She paused, revolving in her mind Jane's unaccountable behaviour in the Circulating Library on the occasion when they had met Sir Richard there. The girl had acted then as if she had suffered some shock. Could it be that she had previously met and fallen in love with him? It must be so, unlikely as it seemed.

"Where did you first meet Richard!" she asked, her tone sharp.

"It is no matter," replied Jane.

"I see you do not mean to tell me! Perhaps he will be more forthcoming."

"You are welcome to try, if it pleases you," answered Jane, indifferently.

"Be sure I shall! I like not mysteries. But I must confess that I understand your refusal of his proposals even less than before I knew this."

"Very likely," said Jane, drily.

"If you love him, why not take your chance?"

"For reasons of which you know nothing!" cried Jane, goaded beyond endurance. "You are a stranger to any decent feeling, Celia Bordesley, and if you imagine that I mean to remain an hour longer under your roof, you are mistaken!"

Celia recoiled a step, amazed. This was a different Jane from the mild-mannered young woman who had borne her company for the last ten days.

"Since I have been here," went on Jane, with biting emphasis, "I have watched you abuse your position with everyone. You are cruel and domineering with the servants, who cannot answer back; you have tried to taunt and humiliate me, knowing my situation places retaliation out of my power. You are unfaithful to a husband who shows you nothing but kindness; and you toy—" Jane's voice trembled a little "—with the affection of a man who, I am convinced, is essentially honourable."

Celia's glance sharpened at this; but she was still too thunder-struck for speech. Jane's grey eyes flashed like steel as she hurled her final words of contempt.

"I hope that the marriage, which you have made purely for your advancement in the world, may continue to pay you the return you expected: for myself, I would rather have the dreary future you predict for me! At least I have my self-respect!"

With a twist of her light form, she turned and whisked from the room, before Celia could recover sufficiently to utter a word.

My lady remained standing where she was, a cruel smile twisting her red lips. It was all too plain that Jane Tarrant was jealous, believing Sir Richard to be in love with her, Celia. Well, let the little fool think so, if she chose! It was not Celia's intention to enlighten her. If she did so, perhaps

Jane might reconsider her refusal of the gentleman's offer of marriage. This would not suit Celia's book; she had no wish to see Jane's advancement in the world, even though her companion must still be her inferior in rank and fortune. There were too many things that rankled from the long past: Jane's popularity with the other pupils at Miss Leasowe's Seminary, the interest which had attached to her there by reason of her having a dashing Naval officer as father. At that period of her life, Celia had been ever conscious of an inferiority to Jane, an inferiority which she attributed entirely to circumstance. Now at last she felt herself to hold the superior position, and she did not mean to relinquish her advantage.

Meanwhile Jane was enquiring of the servants where she might find the Earl. In the white heat of her anger, she meant to seek him out at once, and inform him that she intended to quit his service immediately. She must leave this house without delay—this hateful house where she had lost the tranquillity which it had taken her so long to attain after her father's death. Nothing now could ever be quite the same, she told herself despairingly; but at least she could cut herself off from all the torture of future meetings with Sir Richard, of hearing his name spoken, and of being in the same house as his mistress.

She was informed that his lordship was risen, and could be found in the library. She turned her course that way, and, knocking briefly on the door, entered.

My lord was standing before the table, looking down at a large volume which lay open upon it. He looked up at Jane's entrance, and raised his brows.

"Good morning, Miss Tarrant. I trust you slept well?"

"Indifferently, I thank you, my lord. There is something I must say to you, if you can spare me a moment."

The green eyes flickered.

"By all means. Let us be seated."

He waved his hand towards a chair.

"I prefer to stand, my lord. What I have to say will not take long. I wish to leave your service."

He raised his quizzing glass, and surveyed deliberately, but not offensively, her flushed cheeks and eyes which flashed fire.

"You appear to be in some heat, Miss Tarrant," he said, languidly. "A quarrel with Celia, perhaps? Do not regard it—it will pass."

"I have reasons—pressing personal reasons—for wishing to be released immediately," insisted Jane, compressing her lips.

"What has she said to you, my dear? Some piece of feminine malice, I doubt not. But you are too sensible to be driven away by such shifts. You know how I rely upon you."

"I am sorry if you do, my lord," replied Jane, in a quieter tone. "But I find that I am not suited to this post. I ask your leave to go today—now."

"And if I refuse?"

He dropped the eyeglass, regarding her with a speculative smile.

She shook her head. "I can brook no refusal, my lord."

He raised his brows.

"This is high-handed indeed."

"I have the right of any human being to speak my mind when I am driven past endurance," said Jane, with rising anger.

He nodded. "To be sure, you have rights, indeed—more, perhaps, than you know of; but what is all this about being driven past endurance?"

She raised her eyes to his face. As once before, when the green and grey eyes met, something stirred between them.

"I cannot tell you, my lord," she said, and there was regret in her voice. Unaccountably, she suddenly felt that she would have liked to confide in him. "To do so would entail speaking of matters which are not mine to reveal."

"Do not concern yourself," he answered, gently. "Perhaps I understand better than you believe possible."

On a sudden, he moved across the room, and took both her hands in his.

"I cannot keep you here against your will, Jane: it must be for you to decide. Nevertheless, I beg you to stay—for my sake."

She started, withdrawing her hands from his.

"What are you saying, my lord? I do not understand—"

"I am saying that I have come to value you, Jane, in the time that you have been in this house; to feel for you all that affection which once, long ago, I had for another object—long since removed from my sight, alas, and never truly valued at its worth while there was yet time. Other kinds of love I have known indeed, and it was one of these which led me into the marriage which from the first I knew in my heart was worthless. Yet it was not until I brought you here that I fully realised just how impossible it was ever to hope for happiness from my union with Celia. You have taught me that, dear Jane, in teaching me to love you."

CHAPTER XIX

THE STORY OF ARABELLA

FOR A moment, Jane stood rooted to the spot in horror. This was the final disaster; already she had endured so much today. She had received an offer of marriage from the man whom she loved, but could not accept; she had been taunted unbearably by Celia, and obliged to give up her post without any immediate prospect of obtaining another; and now, the last straw, here was the Earl of Bordesley proposing to her she dared not imagine what. Indignation finally superseded all other emotions, and she turned upon him vehemently.

"How dare you speak to me in that wanton, wicked way! Had I anyone to protect me—"

Her voice choked on a sob. A look of alarm came over the Earl's features, and he took a quick step towards her. She backed away, and turned to fly his presence.

"No, stop!"

The sharp command halted her at the door. She half turned to face him.

"You have me wrong, my child. I am not proposing anything dishonourable to you. But it is my own fault: I am forgetting that you are not as well-informed as I. Come here, Jane; I have something to show you."

She started to comply with the request, then halted irresolutely.

"Come!" he said, persuasively. "This is something you must know. You need have no fear of me; I will not molest you."

Her alarm quietened at his tone, and curiosity overcame her caution. She approached the table where he was standing. He was staring down at the open book which lay there, and at the portrait which was on top of it. Jane recognised it for the one she had discovered the night before. The merry, elfin face met her gaze with a twinkle that seemed to come to life.

"I'd forgotten where this was hid," said the Earl, in a pensive tone of voice. "Then I suddenly recollected how fond she

147

was of this book, and that I'd placed this one picture here at the time when my father had them all destroyed. You will be wondering who she is, Jane. It is my sister, Arabella."

All Jane's disquiet had by now slipped away from her, for the Earl's manner was abstracted, scarcely conscious any longer of the girl at his side. Slowly his lips formed sentences that brought to life the past.

"Yes, little Bella—bright, gay, volatile as quicksilver, worshipped by my father. My mother died giving birth to her, and afterwards the child filled his heart. I was ten years older than she, and off to school while she was still in leading-strings. Our ways did not often cross, yet I, too, was her slave. I think as she grew older, every man was at her feet: but there was only one who ever stood any chance with her."

He broke off, and touched the portrait lightly with his fingers, as though caressing the red-gold hair.

"He was a midshipman of good, though impecunious family. God knows how she ever met him, but Bella had a way of her own: not for nothing was she born with this red hair. My father had made his plans for her future from the day she was twelve years old. She was to wed with the Duke of Norton, thus uniting two great titles and fortunes. During the next six years, he came to consider this scheme as a thing accomplished in all but fact."

He stopped for a moment, sighed, and went on again.

"I was at home on the day when this sailor fellow waited on my father to ask permission to pay his addresses to Bella. I understand that he afterwards fought many a gallant action, but that, surely, was his most courageous deed. Bella came to me, and told me that he intended to come that morning. I asked her if the fellow was mad. 'Mad or not, you may be sure I mean to have him!' she answered me, and I saw from her face that she would stop at nothing. I had seen that look before. He came—a handsome lad, if my memory serves me; I think we should have dealt well with each other, had our ways been fated to lie together. My father took a horsewhip to him, and locked Bella in her room. By nightfall, she had got out somehow, and was gone. She left a letter telling my father that both she and her lover considered that he had forfeited any right to her duty, and that they intended to marry without his consent."

"She was right!" exclaimed Jane, her eyes shining, caught up in the story.

"You think so?" For a moment, he regarded her gravely;

then turned his eyes back to the picture. "She would have been glad to hear you say it."

His face was sad now, and his voice sank a little.

"We never saw her again," he continued. "She wrote to us from time to time, but my father tore the letters across and threw them in the fire without so much as opening them. On the night when we discovered her gone, he went round the house removing all traces of her presence—tearing down and burning portraits, instructing that all her personal effects be buried at the farthest point of the grounds, even shooting her little dog. He was like one possessed. I tried to reason with him, and he struck me—I left the house, and did not return for months, until he had begged my pardon. This one picture of her I had in a drawer in my own room; it had lately been drawn by a lady of my acquaintance. I dared not leave it there, for I was frequently from home, and feared that some abigail would find it in my absence, and take it to my father. I put it in this book, knowing it would be tolerably safe there; my father was not a reading man—the same, I fear, is true of me."

He lifted the portrait from the book, and placed it on the table, directly under Jane's gaze. She fastened her eyes on the merry face. Had some premonition of the sad fate of this lovely girl visited her, when first she had seen that face, she wondered? She remembered the chill of the room on that previous occasion, the gentleness which had moved her to lay the picture softly by, as though it were a living thing.

"You will doubtless be wondering," said the Earl, "why I did nothing to get in touch with my sister. I have no valid excuse to plead. I was an indolent, pleasure-loving young man, caught up in the gaieties of the Town; and I possessed no clue to her whereabouts. To have sought her out would have put me to some trouble, and I was too selfish and thoughtless to make the effort. Soon it was too late. A letter came for my father one day, written in a strange hand. It contained the news of her death."

His head was bowed now, and he suddenly seemed to have shrunk and aged. Jane placed her hand gently on his arm, forgetting her former fears.

"I am sorry," she murmured.

Her tone rather than the words conveyed comfort. He covered her hand with his for a moment, then let it fall away.

"There is nothing that haunts a man so much as the things he once might have done, and did not. My father made no reply to the letter, and I never saw it: I was away, and he gave me the news on my return. It stunned me for a time. I could not think her dead—so bright, so vital a being to be extinguished like that in a moment."

He stopped. A long silence fell over the musty room. Jane shivered, as last she had done when she stood there alone; but it was not cold in the room now.

"Many years passed," he went on, at last. "I became increasingly caught up in my own affairs, my father grew old alone, a bitter, brooding man. You may perhaps know that he died a short time since."

He glanced at Jane questioningly. She was seeing in her imagination the old man who had ruthlessly cut himself off from the one thing he loved above all others. She nodded, too moved for speech.

"A few days before his death," continued the Earl, "I believe he knew that his end was near. He sent for me, and told me then that some years back he had received a letter from a lawyer informing him that Arabella's husband had been killed in action. This man had said that their only child, a daughter, was now thrown upon the mercy of the world."

Here he paused, and looked into Jane's face. An awareness came into her eyes, and they slowly filled with tears. He placed a gentle hand on her bright hair.

"My father had, at that time, paid no more attention to this information than he had to the news of my sister's death: when he felt that his last moments had come, he bitterly regretted this fact. He spoke to me of his repentance over his treatment of my sister, and how different his life might have been had he shown her the understanding she surely ought to have been able to count upon from him. He felt very strongly the wrong he had done her, and the love which might have changed his life had he guarded it. His bitterest regret was that he could make no amends to Arabella; but he said that he had provided for her child, having sent for his lawyer, and settled half his fortune upon the unknown girl. He bade me seek her out, and love her if I could, for Bella's sake. He prayed earnestly that I might not be too late, and I should not find the girl fallen upon evil ways."

Jane was sobbing now, quietly, unashamedly. The Earl placed his arm comfortingly about her shoulders.

"I reassured my father as best I might, and set about my task. It was not easy, for he did not remember the lawyer's name, and had not kept the letter. Up to the moment of his death, I had made no headway, and was forced to tell him so. Yet, at the very end, I believe he knew that all would be well: for with his last breath he named my sister, and he passed with a peaceful smile on his lips such as I had not seen for many a long year."

He ceased speaking, and tenderly regarded the girl at his side. After a moment, he produced a lace-bordered handkerchief and gently wiped the tears away from her cheeks, as though she had been a child.

"It all happened a long time ago," he said, softly. "We must believe that they are happy now—even my father."

Jane raised her tear-stained face. He touched the locket at her neck.

"I have often wondered what that contained," he said. "May I not see?"

She put up her hands to unclasp the chain, then, opening the locket, passed it to him.

"It is my father," she said, in a low tone.

He looked full at the proud, handsome head and piercing eyes of the miniature.

"It is very like," he said, quietly, and set the locket down beside the picture of Arabella.

"Let them lie thus awhile, dear child: they were man and wife."

Her eyes sought and held his, and this time she was glad of the warmth that flowed between them.

"Then I am your niece."

There was no surprise in her tone. He raised one eyebrow, and the sadness left his face.

"You had guessed? Yes, I sensed it at some point in my story."

"When you mentioned Mr. Sharratt's letter," said Jane, "I was certain, although I had suspected before. It is just what he would have done. But he knew I was coming here, yet he said nothing to me of all this. Why was that, my lord?"

He took her hand, and carried it gently to his lips.

"Can you not call me uncle? You are very like your mother, Jane, though you have your father's eyes, and the hair which one would expect from a fusion of black and red. Yes, well—this lawyer—he could not tell you, because he did not know."

"Not know?" She was incredulous.

"He knew, of course, that you were my niece. Why he kept silent on that head, I cannot say; you must ask him yourself. But he knew nothing of my father's will, for I took care to tell no one of it. With the aid of my own lawyers, I managed at last to trace you. It was difficult enough, for you had changed your name, and it took time to prove that Jane Spencer was indeed Jane Tarrant. It is ironical to think that my wife could have saved me all my trouble. However, I could have no notion of that at the time. I wished to become acquainted with you without your knowing in what relationship I stood to you; so I hit upon the plan of engaging you as a companion for my wife. Poor Jane! It was not, in the event, a happy plan; but, naturally, I had no idea that you had met before. Thus, Jane, I came to love you; and can only hope that, little as I deserve it, you may have some small liking for me."

Jane pressed the hand that still retained hers in its grasp, and bent a warm smile on her uncle, though her lips trembled slightly.

"Ever since I first came here," she said, "I've felt that a strange bond existed between us. It used to make me uneasy, but now I understand."

"May that bond grow ever stronger," he answered fervently.

He picked the locket up from the table, and fastened it about Jane's neck.

"And now, my dear," he said, "that you know in what relationship we stand to one another, is there anything more that you feel able to tell me of your reasons for wishing to quit this house?"

Jane hesitated. She would have liked to forge a stronger link between them by confiding in him completely, by asking his advice, even seeking his comfort. But once again she was faced with the impossibility of saying anything without betraying Celia and Sir Richard.

It seemed, however, that there was no need of words between them. He glanced shrewdly into her eyes, and knew her decision.

"I see you will not speak," he said, in a disappointed tone.

"Forgive me if you can—there are obstacles—"

"Not of your making?"

She nodded.

"I understand. What of this fellow Carisbrooke, and that Cheltenham tragedy my wife enacted me last night?"

She hesitated a moment, then answered him in a low voice that was not quite steady.

"I—I love him. That much I may tell you, at least."

"And he?"

She was silent.

"You are no dowerless girl, now, you know," he reminded her, "but an heiress."

Still she made no answer.

"If that story that Celia told me was true," he said, with a slight emphasis, "there is now nothing that need stand in your way."

"Forgive me, my l—uncle," she amended hastily. "Do not press me to speak at this moment, I beg of you. The time may perhaps come—but indeed, I am resolved to put the past behind me, and I cannot do so unless I go away. Now that I have no fear of being an encumbrance, I think I shall avail myself of Mr. and Mrs. Sharratt's kind offer to have me as their guest."

"An encumbrance!" he exclaimed, struck by the word. "Who the devil says so?"

Jane smiled, "No one but myself. You see, while I was poor, I could not accept hospitality from my friends, but now—"

"Now you will give it," he promised, with an answering smile. "We must hold a ball for you, my dear, as soon as the period of mourning is past. And, of course, you must be presented at Court. But all that will have to wait for a while."

In spite of herself, a light came into Jane's eyes, and, for a moment, the Earl caught a glimpse of the vanished madcap Bella.

"That is how you should look," he said, approvingly.

"Such things ought not to count, I know," said Jane, with a smile, "but how delightful it all does sound, to be sure!"

Her expression sobered again.

"There are some difficulties ahead, I fear," she said, hesitatingly.

"Difficulties? I do not perceive any. You are my niece, and will take your proper place in the world."

Jane continued to look uneasy.

"What is it, my dear?" he asked, gently.

"I do not see—, forgive me, sir, but I cannot endure to be under the same roof as—as Celia. I fear it will be necessary for me to make my home elsewhere."

He glanced swiftly at her, then veiled his eyes.

"Do not trouble your head over that," he said, cryptically.

"This lawyer of yours—I must see him to make arrangements for your fortune to be placed at your disposal. Will you ask him to wait upon me at an early date?"

Jane promised, and the Earl crossed to the bell-rope.

"Well, I suppose I must spare you to these people, if that is your wish, but I make no apology for grudging the concession. I have been too long without you to wish to be parted from you so soon. I would accompany you to this man's chambers myself, but that I have an engagement for this morning that cannot wait. However, I will order the carriage to take you there—shall we say in half an hour?"

"I believe half that time should suffice," said Jane with a smile. "My possessions are soon packed."

"That is another matter we shall alter," he replied. "Do not be too long away, child. I shall miss you sadly."

CHAPTER XX

BEAUTY DESTROYED

As THE carriage moved away from the house in Grosvenor Square, Jane's heart lifted with pleasure. It was a lovely day; April's green hand was at last pushing winter firmly away. The gardens of the Square were daubed with touches of yellow and mauve, the birds were singing from the budding branches of the trees. Hope sprang suddenly afresh; the past was left behind, and, whatever hurt she had suffered, time must eventually heal. A little regret must always remain, but a few days spent with the Sharratts would restore at least the outward appearance of equanimity. For the future, she must help herself; courage would be needed, but she did not lack that quality.

Her optimistic mood lasted until the carriage had turned into Brook St., and was approaching Letty's house. The memory of her visit there earlier in the day came back to torment her, and she found her heart beating fast. As the vehicle drew level with the house, she suddenly espied her friend coming down the steps to the street, attended by an abigail. At the same moment, Letty caught sight of her, and signalled impatiently to her to stop. Jane gave the order, and lowered the window as Letty approached the carriage.

"My dearest Jane, I must speak with you!" she began, breathless with excitement. "There is something you must know! Where are you bound?"

Jane explained briefly that she was on an errand to Chancery Lane, not wishing to be more explicit in the hearing of the servants.

"Then I will come with you!" announced Letty. "May I?"

She waited only for Jane's nod, before turning to dismiss her abigail. The steps were let down, and she hastily ascended, seating herself beside Jane on the handsome red leather upholstery of the interior with a sigh of relief. She was silent until the door was closed on the two young ladies, and the

155

carriage moved forward at the sedate pace proper to my lord Bordesley's town coach.

"I was just about to call on you," explained Letty, "in spite of the fact that I might have had the ill-fortune to run across Celia! I could not wait another moment to hear your account—Jane, Richard has told me all!"

Jane glanced at her friend in dismay, but she had no time to make any remark, for Letty plunged headlong into her tale.

"After you left us this morning, Richard went out to keep some appointment or other, and when he returned later he seemed very thoughtful and abstracted. We were alone, for Mama was gone to take luncheon with Mrs. Wyme—she is an old friend of Mama's, but that is nothing to the purpose—anyway, I began to tease him about all his mysteries and silences, for you cannot conceive how trying I have found it, Jane! I thought he might only give me one of his set-downs, for he has the greatest dislike of my taking too much interest in his affairs; but, believe me I was never so much surprised in my life! He suddenly said, 'Very well, Letty, I will tell you all about it, for it will be a relief to me to confide in somebody.' He then went on to say something of what he would do to me if I went blabbing to anyone else— you can imagine the kind of thing!"

"Then you had much better not tell me any more," said Jane, hastily.

"Pooh, no, how could he mean you, for you are most nearly concerned in the whole business, and already know the half, in any case? But only listen, Jane, and do not interrupt."

Jane's lips twitched at this reprimand, but she held her peace.

"Upon my word, I do not rightly know where to begin— but perhaps I should do as he did, and start with the letter."

Jane looked up sharply at this.

"It seems that some little while back, Celia sent for Riccy, and asked him to procure a letter for her from Julian Summers—I don't know if you are acquainted with him, Jane, but he is one of those handsome, dangerous men—anyway, he must be a monster, for he was extorting money from her in exchange for this indiscreet note which she had written to him at some time or other; but I am sure she deserves no better! At that time, Mr. Summers was at his place in Kent, where he always goes when he is in deep water, which is four or five times a year, if all the rumours are true. Anyway,

Richard agreed to take the money to him there, and bring back the letter in exchange."

Jane changed colour, and opened her lips to speak, but no sound came. Letty glanced curiously at her before continuing.

"Richard says he knows he was a fool to let himself get embroiled in Celia's affairs; but he is so good, Jane, and you may know how Celia can wheedle! Anyway, he went on this errand, obtained the letter, and placed it in his snuff box. It is a special kind—it was my grandpapa's—and has a secret compartment in the base, just large enough to contain a small document. He began his journey home, and then the odd part of the story comes in!"

She paused for breath, but this time, Jane did not interrupt. Her heart was surging with thankfulness. So the letter had not been written to Sir Richard, after all—he was not Celia's lover! His clandestine meetings with her were no doubt concerned only with the recovery of the lost letter. And she, Jane, had been in possession of it all the time!

"A mile or so from Mr. Summers' house, Richard was attacked and robbed of all he carried on him. He is quite clear on this, though not on anything that follows for some hours; for, believe it or not, Jane, he has no recollection whatever of what befell him after the attack, until he suddenly found himself in a street down in the City! And that was the next day, mark you!"

She paused here, expecting Jane to exclaim in surprise; but to her amazement, Jane sat there quietly smiling as though she found nothing wonderful in this recital.

"Upon my word, Jane, you take my news very calmly!" exclaimed Letty, in some chagrin.

"I suppose it must seem so to you: but I have a reason. What you tell me of your brother's errand to Kent is news to me, but the rest of the story I know more of than he does himself."

Letty turned an incredulous look upon her friend. Jane proceeded to explain her part in the affair: as she told her story, a weight seemed to slide from her shoulders. It was so much more comfortable not to be obliged to have any more secrets from Letty.

"Well!" exclaimed her friend, when she had come to the end of her story. "And to think that you had Richard's snuff box all the time! But why did you not return it to him, Jane? That I cannot understand."

It was not easy to answer this question without betraying

the one secret which must still be guarded. Jane stumbled a little over her words.

"He did not remember me—it would have been necessary to explain how I came by it, and I did not wish him to feel under any obligation to me—my situation altogether was so difficult—"

Her voice tailed off. Letty gave her a shrewd glance; she knew her Jane.

"Oh, yes, I begin to see how it is!" she said, causing Jane to blush. "But you would have saved him a power of trouble—and Celia, too, though I don't care a fig for her! However, they were both at their wits' end, trying to discover where the letter could be; Riccy says that he even tried breaking into Mr. Summers' town house in an endeavour to find it! But although he did not succeed, he did have a talk with the man Summers, and it seems that they both came to the conclusion that—this, at any rate, you cannot know, Jane—Mr. Summers' valet and Celia's abigail were concerned in the business. It seems that this girl Betty overheard Richard's conversation with Celia when first he talked with her about the letter, and Betty thought it a splendid opportunity for enriching herself, so she put the valet up to stealing the letter; only it went wrong, and instead the man planned to hold Richard up on his way back to London, and take the letter from him. Their plans seem to have been doomed to failure, do they not, for that went wrong, too?"

Jane nodded absently. She had wondered about Betty's part in last night's scene. Here then was the explanation.

"Anyway," continued Letty, enjoying her role of informant, "when Riccy went to see Celia yesterday evening, he told her what they suspected, and she taxed Betty with it. Apparently Celia lost her temper with the maid, and that brought on the dreadful scene in which you took part, Jane. There is no need to tell you of that, for you know it already. It was most unfortunate that the Earl should have walked in just then—but how like Celia to make up such a wicked lie to account for Richard's presence in her room!"

Jane did not reply. There was so much in what she had just learned to make her thankful, so many points on which this information showed Sir Richard in a new light; her mind was too occupied for comment. Luckily, Letty did not appear to feel the lack of it.

"There is more, Jane. After Richard left my lord's house last night, he encountered the abigail, who was running away.

He forced her to admit that what he suspected was true, and made her promise to take him to the valet, Perkins. The meeting was arranged for this morning, but first I came to bring you to see Riccy."

The colour flamed again in Jane's face as she recalled the interview.

"You know your own business best, to be sure, Jane; but I am persuaded that Richard is more than half taken with you already, in spite of the fact that he does not realise you have met before! However, perhaps you are indifferent to him."

This remark was accompanied by a sly, sideways glance. What Letty saw on her friend's face brought a smile to her generous mouth.

"When you went away," continued Letty, "Richard went to keep his appointment with the man Perkins. He succeeded in recovering all his property except the snuff box, and apparently Perkins swore by all that is holy that he knew nothing of that. Of course, we both know that he was speaking the truth, but Richard could not, and it seems to have taken some time to convince him."

She broke off, and a fierce expression crossed her normally gentle, good-humoured face.

"If only I could have laid hands on that man—! However, I believe Richard may have succeeded in giving him a good fright!"

"I have no doubt of it," said Jane, conjuring up a mental image of Sir Richard's heavy dark brows and broad shoulders. He would be a fearsome man in anger, she surmised.

"Riccy forced Perkins to tell him the name of the inn where his horse had been left—the very inn, Jane, where you and Riccy met! And that is where he has gone now—he went as soon as he had finished telling me the whole story, not staying for anything but to push a few clothes into a bag. He said that he is determined to remain there until he has found his snuff box, and cleared up the mystery that surrounds those hours which he has forgotten. He made up his mind that the box must have been dropped somewhere near the spot where he was attacked, and feels that the inn will be a likely starting point for his inquiries."

"So it will be," replied Jane, "for I showed the box to the landlord's wife as proof that your brother would be able to meet his reckoning. She would not be likely to forget such a handsome trinket."

"But what are we to do, Jane?" exclaimed Letty. "We

know that he can never find it there. We cannot leave him in ignorance!"

"The box is soon obtained, at any rate," answered Jane. "I left it in Mr. Sharratt's keeping, as I told you, and you may have it of him when we arrive in Chancery Lane."

"But what of Richard? He may remain in Kent for days, searching and questioning to no purpose, while we hold the key to the riddle! Jane, can we not go after him and explain?"

Jane hesitated.

"Why, yes, I think if I were you I should go, Letty."

"But why cannot you—oh, of course! I am forgetting your situation with regard to Celia Bordesley! Do not return there, Jane; come with me to Kent—I assure you, there is not the least need for you to concern yourself with your future—"

Jane interrupted her, smiling.

"No, there is not, Letty. I have something surprising to tell you. This is a day of confidences for you, it seems."

She went on to tell her friend of the change in her fortunes. Letty listened thunderstruck, for once forbearing to interrupt. Amazement at last gave place to delight.

"My dearest Jane!"

Warm arms encircled Jane's neck, and for a time everything else was forgotten in the wonder of this latest piece of news. But at last Letty's eager questions were all answered, and she could really believe in Jane's changed state.

"It is just what I have always been planning for you, only a great deal better!" she cried. "And it has fallen out very fortunately for my purpose, for now there is nothing to hinder you from accompanying me into Kent at once!"

Jane was silent for so long, that her friend looked at her in surprise.

"Indeed, Letty," she began falteringly, at last, "I scarcely know what to say—I am already engaged to spend a visit of some days to Mr. and Mrs. Sharratt, as I told you—I don't quite see how I may come with you."

"That is not spoken like my Jane!" cried Letty, indignantly. "You wretch, I believe you are making excuses! You also told me that you had but just formed the intention of going to the Sharratts, and therefore they cannot be expecting you; so what is to prevent your going there in a day or two, instead of immediately? No, Jane, you must do better than that, if you hope to take me in!"

Jane smiled wryly, and looked guilty.

"That is true," she acknowledged. "I am sorry, Letty, but I—indeed, I had much rather not come, if you will forgive me. I—"

She stopped, unable to put into words her real reason for being unwilling to accompany her friend. However, there was no need; Letty was beginning to have a very fair notion of how matters stood, and meant to do her best to arrange them.

"Then you will come! I knew you could not refuse me for long! We must go home straight from your lawyer's, and furnish ourselves with necessaries for a night's stay in Kent—for I suppose we shall not care to make the journey there and back today, although perhaps we might, for it is not much above twenty miles, from what Richard told me."

Jane found herself unwillingly committed to the plan: she had no objection to postponing her visit to the Sharratts, or accompanying Letty, but dreaded another interview with Sir Richard. To return his snuff box would involve her in explanations which would be difficult to make without betraying her feelings. If only he could remember the whole thing for himself, it would be easier: but to be obliged to tell him of the bargain they had made, to remind him of the service, small though it was, that she had done him, these were considerations that weighed heavily on Jane's mind. It was little wonder that the rest of the journey was accomplished in comparative silence.

Once arrived in Chancery Lane, the interview with Mr. Sharratt was as brief as civility would allow. Jane explained the errand on which she and Letty were bound, and her friend's desire for haste. On learning the identity of the mysterious owner of the snuff box, the laywer's relief was evident: he no longer seemed perturbed by Jane's interest in the gentleman. He handed the box over to her keeping, and Jane went on to tell him her news.

His congratulations were warm and heartfelt. She had been a favourite with him since infancy, and he had long grieved over his inability to procure for her what was her right.

"But what I cannot understand, sir," said Jane, after she had thanked him for his kind wishes, "is why you never told me that the Earl was my uncle—for I know that you were aware of it."

"I thought I saw the hand of Providence in the affair," he confessed. "I knew that the Earl must come to value you in time if you were both under the same roof; and it seemed to me that, after a proper interval, I might have discovered your identity to him with some hope of interestiñg him in your welfare. Had I informed you of the relationship, however, I knew that you would in all probability refuse to go to his house, thus foiling my plan. Did I not judge you aright?"

Jane had to acknowledge the truth of this.

"Man proposes," replied the lawyer, "but other hands than mine had your affairs in their direction. Such a reflection must make us humble. However, my dear, I must not detain you now; I will wait on your uncle later in the day, as you tell me that is his desire."

Jane rose to go, and mentioned the matter of her proposed visit. In his dry way, the lawyer was delighted. He felt all the honour of being singled out by the Earl of Bordesley's niece, who might so easily have forgotten her old friends in the heady excitement of being elevated to a new way of life. He assured her of his wife's equal delight in the scheme, and it was arranged that Jane should come to them as soon as she returned from her expedition into Kent.

It only remained for Jane to collect Letty from the clerk's office, where she had waited during this interview, charming even that unimpressionable little man with her blue eyes and merry smile. Once back in the carriage, Letty was all for returning immediately to Brook St., so that they might get started without delay, but Jane demurred.

"I feel that I must first return to my uncle's house, Letty. It is only right that I should inform him of my change of plan. There is another matter, too, which I've been turning over in my mind—don't you think that I perhaps ought to return this letter to Celia? Heaven knows I have no wish ever to set eyes on her again, but the note belongs to her, and will have to be given back eventually. Only imagine her state of mind while she has not known where it may be!"

"Don't expect me to feel sympathy for Celia," said Letty, with a grimace. "However, I dare say you are right, and to confess the truth, I would rather that Richard should not be obliged to see her again to hand it to her. But could we not more simply give it to one of your uncle's servants to deliver?"

Jane shook her head. "I had thought of that, but there is too much risk of it coming to my uncle's hand. I will not have his peace of mind disturbed. No, Letty, I must deliver it in person."

Letty saw that her friend was adamant, and conceded the point, arranging to call later for Jane at the Earl's residence. She was set down in Brook St., and Jane continued on her way alone.

Arrived at the house, her enquiries for her uncle were met with the information that his lordship was out; but my lady was above-stairs, the servant stated, with a look full of some significance that escaped Jane's comprehension. She left a hastily scribbled note for the Earl with the man, and started upstairs to Celia's room.

No answer came to her first hesitant tap upon the door. She waited a moment, then tapped a second time, more loudly. There was still no answer. She fretted a little, mindful of her promise to Letty not to be long about her task. After another purposeful knock, she ventured to open the door, and walk in. As she closed the door behind her, she stood stock still, her glance travelling round the room in horror.

The handsome apartment had been ravaged as though by a horde of vandals. The muslin draperies were torn from the windows, and lay in trailing pink clouds across the carpet. Chairs were overturned, and the striped satin sofa rent from end to end, as though by the fierce claws of a tiger. Scattered all about the room, the torn silk cushions oozed their contents forlornly. Jane raised startled eyes to the overmantel surmounting the fireplace; the glass was splintered, and in the hearth were the shattered fragments of a Dresden shepherdess and a pair of handsome Sèvres vases. Wherever she turned her gaze was ruin and destruction. The boudoir, once a lovely setting for the Incomparable Celia, was now a shambles. Of its occupant, there was no sign.

Fear clutched suddenly at Jane's heart. Her uncle—had he committed some frightful act in one of his fits of jealousy? Had he perhaps discovered that last night's story was false, and that Sir Richard had been with Celia, not herself? Her quick imagination conjured up visions of terror, painting them in lurid colours. Her breath came unsteadily as she hastened towards the door of the bedchamber opening off the boudoir.

It opened as she approached, and Celia came out. Her hair was in some disorder, and her low-cut gown was torn, revealing her white bosom. Relief surged over Jane as a quick glance assured her that Celia was unhurt.

On seeing Jane, she halted, and her face contorted.

"You!" Her tone was low, venomous. "Get out of my sight, you vile bitch!"

Jane stiffened, her alarm giving place to anger. Whatever had befallen Celia, it was obvious that she needed neither help nor pity. For the first time, it occurred to Jane that Celia herself might be responsible for the chaotic state of the room.

"I came to bring you this," she said, coldly, holding out the letter.

"What is it?"

Celia put out her hand gropingly for the paper, and unfolded it. Jane intended to go then, but some impulse in which curiosity had a part, kept her there. Celia stared at the note in a dazed way for some moments, as though unable to understand what it was. At last, she let it drop from her hand to the floor, and broke into peal after peal of high-pitched, hysterical laughter.

"So you bring me the letter—you, of all people!" she shrieked, a horrible laugh punctuating her utterance. "The letter for which I risked so much—the letter which Francis mustn't see—the letter—the letter—"

Her words were lost in a cacophony of wild sounds.

Jane had instinctively stepped back a pace at the onset of this outburst, but now, fearing that Celia might go into a fit, she nerved herself to move towards my lady, and slap her sharply across her cheek.

Celia choked on a laughing shriek. For several moments, she stood staring at Jane with vacant eyes: then suddenly she collapsed in a heap on to the flooor, shaking with sobs.

"Celia—for Heaven's sake, what has happened?" cried Jane, thoroughly alarmed.

"Happened?" sobbed Celia, incoherently. "What has happened? My ruin has happened, that's what!"

She raised a ravaged face to Jane, and went on in a high, fierce tone, but more intelligibly than before.

"My precious Francis has turned me off like any servant—to be sure, he is to pay me a handsome allowance, but what's that to being a Countess, and having all the Bordesley fortune at my command: And I may not live in Town any longer, not that I would wish to, for none would receive me now! The letter—I thought that if only I could keep the letter from Francis, I might be safe, fool that I was! I had everything so nicely planned—you, Richard, Julian, Francis, all were pawns in my game—but I reckoned without that foul slut, Betty!"

Hereupon, she let out such a horrible string of abuse that Jane turned hastily to leave.

"Ay, go!" shrieked Celia, hurling after her one of the torn cushions, there being no more lethal weapon to hand. "Go, and may you rot in hell!"

Jane ran from the room, and shut the door thankfully behind her. Once outside, she could go no farther for a moment, and stood still, one hand leaning upon the door-knob. She was trembling from head to foot, and her knees felt ready to give under her. It had been startling to witness the ruin of that once immaculate room; but the change in its owner had shocked her profoundly.

Unsteadily, she made her way downstairs. The servant glanced sharply at her face, and asked if he should summon an abigail to her assistance. Jane shook her head.

"No, thank you," she answered, weakly. "I am going out again immediately. You will not forget my note for his lordship?"

The man promised, and opened the door for her to pass out into the street. She was slowly descending the steps just as the Carisbrooke carriage drew up outside the house.

Letty exclaimed in alarm at sight of her friend's pale face, and quickly drew her into the coach. Jane succumbed gratefully to the warm arms, and burst into helpless tears.

"Why, what can be amiss, Jane? Dear Jane, do but tell me!"

Incoherently, Jane repeated the tale.

"But I don't altogether understand—do you weep for Celia? Upon my word, it does you credit if you can feel sympathy for her, for I must confess that, for my part, I am monstrous glad! She deserves it all, as you would think had you seen how she made my brother suffer!"

Jane dried her eyes, a little ashamed now of her outburst.

"No, Letty, it isn't that."

She paused for a minute, to collect herself, then went on; "As you say, one cannot feel sorry for Celia; she has done too much harm. But somehow, I grieve for what she might have been—I never could bear to see the destruction of a lovely thing, and Celia was a lovely woman, who might have brought so much happiness to others, to my uncle—perhaps, once, to your brother. Do you remember how, when we were children, Letty, we believed utterly that goodness must lie behind a lovely face? It must be many years since we realised the folly of such a belief, yet even now, one cannot help hoping—she was so beautiful—surely she must have been created for something better than this?"

Letty nodded sympathetically, for once allowing her friend to run on uninterrupted. Jane was normally so reserved, yet Letty knew her feelings to be perhaps deeper than most: it would be better for her this time to speak freely of them. It had not escaped Letty's notice that Jane spoke of Celia in the past, almost as though she were dead. This was well; it promised that presently Jane might be able to forget my lady Bordesley's part in her own life for ever.

CHAPTER XXI

THE AWAKENING

IT WAS something before four o'clock in the afternoon when Sir Richard arrived at the Three Tuns Inn in Kent. As the curricle drew up in the yard, an ostler came lounging forward, a straw dangling loosely from his mouth. At sight of the sporting equipage and high-bred team, he threw the straw aside, and quickened his pace to a run.

Sir Richard leapt lightly down, gave a few terse instructions to his groom, and directed his steps to the front entrance of the inn. Here he was met by the landlord, who asked how he might be of service to his visitor.

"I shall be staying here for a few days," replied Sir Richard, looking about him without enthusiasm. The place wore that air of clean cheerlessness which is so often the hallmark of an acid housewife. "I take it that you have a vacant bedchamber and a private parlour for my use?"

The landlord replied hastily that he had, and offered to show the rooms to his guest.

"I'll take the bedchamber on trust," said Sir Richard, waving the offer aside, "so long as the sheets be aired. However, you may show me the parlour, and bring a bottle of claret."

The landlord assented, and led the way down a short passage covered with a strip of almost threadbare carpeting, until he arrived at the entrance to the parlour. Here he stood aside for his guest to enter the room.

Sir Richard, however, paused on the threshold, his eyes slowly travelling round the apartment. His glance lingered for some moments on a glass case containing a stuffed fish, which hung over the mantelshelf; then it passed on to the chintz-covered sofa before the fire. He frowned heavily.

The landlord surveyed him anxiously.

"Bain't it to your honour's liking? To be sure, yon fish've happen been 'anging there a few years too many, but my Granfer caught 'un, and we didn't care to get rid o' 'un on

that account. Still, if y'r honour've taken the thing in dislike—"

"No, no," disclaimed Sir Richard, passing a hand across
his brow with a weary gesture. "I was thinking of something
else; it's a very fine fish, I'm sure; leave it be."

He crossed over to the sofa, and began slowly to draw off
his gloves. The landlord prepared to depart; but before he
could reach the door, Sir Richard detained him with a gesture.

"One of my reasons for coming here," he said, "is to
recover a mare of mine which was left in your stables some
weeks since, until I should collect her. I take it that you have
her safe?"

The landlord's broad face clouded with consternation, and
his reply was long in coming.

"Why, yes, y'r honour, there is a horse—leastways, there is
and there isn't—but I'll fetch my missus, she knows all about
it, and I'll bring y'r honour's wine at the same time."

He vanished from the room with commendable speed.

Sir Richard frowned, and once more slowly glanced round
the parlour with a perplexed air. To his knowledge, he had
never before been in this place, and yet—

His meditations were interrupted by the entrance of the
landlord's wife, a woman of vinegary aspect, which was not
relieved by the ingratiating smile she at present wore.

"My husband says you've come for the mare, your honour.
To be sure, I won't need to keep you waiting for long—she
should be back in an hour or so."

"Back?" queried Sir Richard.

"Well, y'r honour, 'tis a long time we've kept her here, and
his saying she would be called for in a day or two, and leaving only enough money for that length of time; and so, not
knowing as how y'r honour would be calling for her today—
and I'm sure if you'd have sent us a line, we'd have managed
things very differently—I made so bold as to lend her to him
for an hour or so, she being in need of exercise, and him
paying well."

"What's all this?" asked Sir Richard, puzzled by the too
frequent use of pronouns in her speech. "Do I understand
you to say that you've hired my horse out to someone else?"

The woman nodded. "That's it, y'r honour. A gennelman
as lives close by, and has promised faithful to deliver her up
by five o'clock. So, if you'll have the goodness to wait a little,
and perhaps partake of some refreshment—"

"You took too much upon yourself," he began; then paused, recollecting that, after all, the mare had been there some time, and perhaps these people had despaired of ever seeing her claimed.

"Very well," he continued, cutting short the landlady's abject apologies. "You may bring me something to eat."

She turned to obey, thankful to have got over the matter so lightly; but before she reached the door, he addressed her again.

"Stay; there is another matter I would like to question you upon."

She halted, her thin lips fixed in an ingratiating smile. Sir Richard paused, and seemed uncertain whether to continue.

"Have you perchance heard anything of a trinket being picked up hereabouts?" he asked, at last. "A gold snuff box, ornamented with jewels?"

The landlady started, and turning, stared hard at him for a time. Recognition came into her glance.

"Well, I never!" she declared in surprise. "I do believe as you are the very gennelman as was picked up by the roadside unconscious that very same day as the man brought your horse here!"

"What's that?" he asked sharply. "Found unconscious, you say? By whom?"

"Lord, sir, y'r honour must surely remember! A party of people travelling in a stage were stranded here, and they found you and brought you in. There was a snuff box, too— yes, I remember it clearly—sort of tree on it, there was, with fruit all done in rubies and emeralds—the female showed it to me."

"That's the one," he said, quickly. "But what female?"

"Dear, oh, dear, y'r honour can't have forgotten! The female who bathed your head, and took breakfeast with you the next morning! And afterwards you travelled up to Lunnon with her and the rest of 'em in the stage."

Sir Richard passed his hand across his head; something was stirring in his brain.

"What was she like, this lady?" he asked, slowly.

"Land sakes!" The landlady seemed overpowered by his lack of recollection. Most likely he had been drunk, after all, she told herself.

"Why, she was a very ordinary female of about two and twenty, p'raps older, I'm sure! Mind you, I think she was Quality, by the airs she gave herself, but a most ordinary, shabby creature, I assure your honour, not a penny to her name, I don't doubt, and of no account soever! Very like a governess, I shouldn't wonder!"

"You talk too much," he said sternly. "Mind your tongue when you speak of your betters."

"Betters, indeed!" She tossed her head. "That shabby creature wasn't my betters, not though she did scorn to share a bed with two other females, pretending she must sleep downstairs for fear y'r honour should need nursing, says she, though I'm sure I would have worked my fingers to the bone for y'r honour's comfort, and didn't need the likes of her to tell me—"

"That will do," he said, curtly. "What of the snuff box?"

"Why, she offered it to me in payment for your lodging," said the landlady, giving a carefully expurgated version of the event. She resented his reprimand, but had no intention of doing anything to offend what now appeared to be a good customer. "In course, I didn't take it, and afterwards they must have found some money on y'r honour, though, at first, they said there wasn't a penny piece. I remember Molly the kitchenmaid telling me afterwards that she saw you giving the box to the fem—the lady—next morning, when you was having breakfast together, and she had gone in to clear the table. I suppose only she knows what happened to it after that," she finished, with a malicious sniff.

He stared at her for some moments in a way that quite frightened her.

"Yes, I see," he said slowly, abstractedly.

He began to pace about the room. She watched him in silence, uncertain whether or not to go.

"Will there be anything more, y'r honour?" she ventured, at last.

"What? Oh, no: that is all—but stay—this lady—I accompanied her on the stage coach to London, you say?"

The woman assented, eyeing him strangely: and, her husband arriving at that moment with the wine that had been ordered, she quickly took the opportunity of leaving her disturbing guest. To be sure, it was a dreadful thing that such a fine-looking young man should hit the bottle to the extent that he could not afterwards recollect what he had done! But there was no gainsaying the wildness of some members of the Quality!

When at last he was left completely alone in the parlour, Sir Richard seated himself upon the sofa, and thoughtfully raised his glass to the light. As he gazed at the red wine it held, seeing yet unseeing, he suddenly knew that once before he had sat here in this very room and looked into the red depths of—something, but what? Not a glass of wine, he felt sure.

He meditated a while, twirling the stem of the glass absently in his fingers. His glance turned from the direction of the small latticed window of the room, and fixed itself on the fire. An awareness crept over him, a strong recollection of a mood rather than an incident: he had sat here once before, gazing into the fire, hopeless, dejected, awaiting someone who to him meant hope and courage.

Who could it have been? He strove to remember, but memory would not be forced. By the landlady's account, it must have been this girl, the supposed governess. He tried to recall her face, but in vain; even the remembered mood was vanishing now, as though he were awaking from a dream. Yet somewhere in the back of his consciousness he knew the landlady's account to be the truth. Why, then, would it not come back to him sharp and clear, as much more distant events in his life would do? The pictures were there, he felt convinced, but they would not swim into focus; they were as reflections on the water with rippling edges not clearly defined, scarce recognisable for the things they were.

He drained his glass suddenly at a gulp, and pushed it away from him, rising impatiently to his feet. He would go out and walk for a while, try to straighten his thoughts. Here in this inn, memories pressed too closely upon him for recognition. With a quick stride, he passed from the room, down the passage, and out into the road.

It was some two hours later when Letty and Jane arrived at the inn. The journey had been accomplished without incident, and almost without conversation; for Letty was deep in hatching schemes for an outcome of this affair that would be to her liking, while Jane's thoughts were equally absorbing. Daylight was beginning to fade as they arrived; birds were singing their last throaty calls, and a little chill had crept into the air.

Jane shook herself out of her abstraction as they passed through the door of the inn into the hall. The landlady was waiting there, and, for a moment, Jane wondered if the woman would recognise her. She gave no sign of doing so, and this Jane attributed to the dim light indoors, for the lamps were not yet kindled. She could not realise how greatly she was changed from the shabby, severe-looking governess who had last passed that way.

Letty inquired for her brother, and Jane's heart began to beat uncomfortably fast. In a moment, she would be face to face with Sir Richard. She knew a sudden onset of panic. Why, oh, why had she allowed Letty to persuade her to come? What was she to say to him, how to act?

She heard the landlady replying that Sir Richard was not at present within; her fears subsided like an outgoing tide.

"My brother out?" Letty was asking, incredulously.

"Yes, ma'am. Been gone nigh on two hours, he has, and his dinner spoiling in the oven. But if you please to come in and wait, ma'am, I'll wager he'll soon be back, for hunger brings a man home sooner than anything else I know of. I'll show you to the parlour, ma'am. Will you be wanting dinner, too?"

"Oh, yes, if you please," replied Letty. "But we will wait in here—it affords a view of the road."

She pushed open the door of the coffee-room as she spoke, and she and Jane entered. As soon as they were alone, she turned an anxious face towards her friend.

"Two hours, Jane, did you hear what she said? Can you imagine where he could go that would detain him all that time? Do you suppose he may have gone to Farrowdene? But why? Mr. Summers is not in residence, and besides, he can hope to learn nothing new there, for he told me that he could remember perfectly all that part of his journey. It was what passed after he had left the house that he could not recollect. Whatever can have become of him, Jane?"

"He is probably trying to retrace the way he took on that previous occasion," said Jane. "In any event, I should not worry. He will return presently, I am sure."

"But I must worry," insisted Letty, fidgetting with her bonnet strings as she peered out of the window. "When one recalls what happened to him before, one cannot but feel anxious!"

"Such a thing couldn't possibly happen again," replied Jane. "It would be stretching coincidence too far."

Her thoughts were not as easy as her words. She was remembering the last time that Sir Richard had vanished from the place where she had expected him to be. On that occasion, the events of the preceding hours had been erased from his memory. Had a similar calamity befallen him again?

Was he perhaps wandering about helplessly at this very moment, not knowing who he was nor whence he came?

She did her best to push such thoughts away. On no account must she allow Letty to guess at them. Her friend was already sufficiently perturbed in imagining her brother to have been set upon again. That was extremely unlikely; but this other hazard was much more probable, and what would her friend's state of mind be if it once occurred to her?

The minutes passed slowly. Some attempts were made at conversation, but these were merely desultory remarks thrown into the void of silence to stop the ever quickening flow of alarming thought and surmise. Letty sat on the window seat, staring out into the road through the gathering dusk, tying and untying her bonnet strings ceaselessly with trembling fingers. Jane stood motionless beside her, outwardly as controlled as ever.

Twenty minutes or more must have gone by in this way, when suddenly Letty started and jumped to her feet. A figure had just come into view, striding up the road in the direction of the inn, with the gait of a healthy, able-bodied man. She knew him instantly; and, with a glad little cry, she rushed from the room, and out into the road towards him, leaving the door of the coffee-room open in her haste.

Relief flooded over Jane, and was instantly replaced by a wild confusion. He was here, and safe, and in a moment would be in the room, speaking to her. She could not move, and stood fixed to the spot, staring from the window at the meeting of brother and sister. She saw the joyful look on Letty's face, and the astonishment of his. They stood there for a while, deep in conversation; and then they started towards the inn. They passed close to the window, but did not notice Jane standing there; presently she heard their steps in the passage, and their voices floated in to her through the open door.

"But who is with you child?" Jane heard him ask. "Not, I hope, Mama?"

"Goodness, no, Riccy, how can you think of such a thing? I would not trouble Mama! No, Jane is with me—Miss Tarrant, you know."

"Miss Tarrant!"

Jane heard the dismay in his voice, and clenched her hands tightly together. He evidently did not wish to see her, was regretting already the impulsive offer he had made to her this morning. Well, he had nothing to fear, she would not remind him of it. Only she wished that she had a little more time to collect herself; she could not face him immediately—just a few more moments . . .

She heard them enter the room, heard the man's swift intake of breath, and startled exclamation as he perceived her standing there at the window in the gathering dusk.

"Good God! The dream!"

She could not understand his words, but believed that she must not have heard them aright. In the present tumult of her feelings, anything was possible. She forced herself to turn, and gave a formal curtsey: words would not come.

"Miss Tarrant!" he said, in tones of deep disappointment. "No, it can't be!"

Under his fixed, perplexed gaze her eyes dropped. No one moved or spoke for what seemed an eternity.

"That figure at the window," he muttered, as though talking to himself; "I could not be deceived. I have seen it too often in my dreams for that. No, it was the same—and yet—"

The room was silent, pressing in upon them. At last, he turned to his sister.

"I have remembered everything," he said. "While I was out walking, bit by bit it all fell into place. I was found unconscious close to this inn by a party of stage travellers; there was a governess among them who tended me. When I discovered that I'd lost my memory, she helped me to get to Town to see her lawyer; but I never saw him, after all, for I recovered my memory while I was waiting alone outside his chambers. In remembering who I was, I forgot again the incidents through which I had recently passed, only to recover them today. I forgot, too, what was most valuable to me to remember—the governess, her name, her face."

He stopped abruptly, and looked from his sister to Jane, who still stood motionless before the window.

"Only that dream was left as a reminder of her," he said, slowly, "though at the time, I could not read its message. But now, today, as I entered this room, the dream came suddenly to life, and there she was, standing at the window. And yet—and yet—I *must* be wrong—"

Letty and Jane said nothing. He stared at the latter with an intense gaze, as though he would penetrate her very soul.

"*Her* name," he said, in a puzzled voice, "was Jane Spencer."

Letty moved towards him, and placed her hand on his arm to claim his attention.

"That is Jane's name," she said, softly. "Jane Spencer Tarrant."

A long silence fell over the room. Jane was certain that the others must hear the tumultuous beating of her heart. Letty looked from one to the other for a moment, then slipped quietly from the room, closing the door firmly behind her. She was not needed there; they did not even notice her going.

"So you are Jane Spencer," said Sir Richard, in a wondering tone, and he moved closer to Jane so that he might better see her face in the fading light. She nodded, and the flickering firelight momentarily caught the burnished gleam of her hair. He reached out, and took one of the bright ringlets in his fingers, twining it as though absently.

"But your hair is different."

She managed to find her voice at that. "You didn't like my hair as it was; I thought perhaps you were right. I—I changed it."

"Did you then care for my opinion?"

Jane could find no ready answer to this. He looked into her face again, releasing the curl reluctantly.

"The eyes are the same—yes, I distinctly remember them."

They lowered before his gaze, and a blush came to Jane's cheek. She hoped that it might escape his notice in the dim light of the room, and sought to provide a distraction.

"You may remember that I have some property of yours."

With unsteady fingers, she took the snuff box from her reticule, and held it out to him. He took it, and laid it carelessly on the window seat, his eyes still on her face.

"I remember also that I am in your debt," he answered, his voice deep.

"That is nothing—do not let us speak of it," she said, uncertainly.

"Presently, perhaps. First there is something I would like you to tell me."

His tone was more assured now; he was rapidly becoming master of the situation, while Jane felt it to be slipping more and more from her grasp. What would he ask her? There were so many awkward questions he might put.

"Why did you not return the snuff box to me before this, I wonder?"

Here it was, the one question she had feared. She answered warily.

"You did not appear to remember me," she said. "At first, the notion crossed my mind that you might not wish to continue the acquaintance."

He started at this, and a look of reproach came into his eyes. Jane's conscience pricked her; what she had said was not strictly true, but somehow she must stop him from guessing at her real reason for failing to return the box. She hurried on with her explanation.

"Later," she said, "when I realised the truth, I was uncertain what was best to be done. It seemed better to wait and see if you would recover your memory, and so I left the box with my lawyer."

He was silent for some minutes after this, and Jane felt that he was weighing the adequacy of her reply. Her uneasiness increased.

"So at first you believed me an ingrate," he said, drily. "I thank you."

"How could I know what to think?" asked Jane, a hint of pleading in her tone. "Your sudden disappearance in Chancery Lane upset all my previous notions—and, besides, Mr. Sharratt and I found the letter in the snuff box. We read it, not realising the nature of it until it was too late. We had hoped thereby to trace you."

"You read Celia's note?" he asked, in alarm.

She nodded, not knowing what to say.

His face darkened. "Small wonder, then, that you should have been so contemptuous towards me this morning. I knew, of course, that you were bound to suspect, from the evidence—but the note would clinch the business for you; naturally, you believed it to have been written to me."

"What else could I think? And yet—"

"A fine opinion you have been holding of me!" he said, bitterly. "An ingrate, and a backstairs lover!"

"Oh, no!"

Jane started forward a step, impulsively. All at once, she felt that it mattered no longer if he should suspect her feelings; the only thing that counted was to remove all traces of the hurt which she saw in his eyes.

"I could never really bring myself to believe either charge," she said, her own eyes soft. "When I thought of your clandestine meetings with Celia, the note—it seemed impossible not to believe the worst: but when I thought of you as I had known you here, for those few short hours—"

He moved towards her, and she hastily drew back a pace.

"Yes, Jane?" he asked, eagerly. "When you thought of that—?"

"I—I could not believe you so base," she murmured, haltingly.

It seemed he had expected another answer, for his disappointment was evident.

"You now know the truth of those meetings with Celia, of course? Letty will have made all clear to you?"

"Yes. I am sorry to have been the unwitting cause of so much trouble. I could not realise how anxiously both you and Celia were seeking the letter. However, she has it safe at last. I delivered it to her myself before Letty and I set out."

She did not mention the scene that had ensued on that occasion, nor her discovery that the Earl of Bordesley was her uncle. Somehow these things seemed to matter very little at present.

"You did?" he exclaimed in relief. "Then the whole wretched business is done with, praise be! When I think of the trouble that accursed letter has caused—"

He broke off, and moved closer to her. It was almost dark now in the room, and his eyes were two deep shadows in his face.

"But I must not curse it too much, after all," he continued, softly, "for without it, I should never have met you."

Jane's bosom rose and fell quickly. Only a step now separated them: suppose she were to sway forward, as she felt that at any minute she must?

"When I asked you to marry me, this morning," said Sir Richard, his tone low and deep, "you told me that there were reasons why such a marriage would be distasteful to you. I want you to tell me what those reasons are."

There was a quiet masterfulness about his manner that would not be denied; his dark eyes compelled hers.

She shook her head, trying to avoid his glance.

"You seemed quite certain that there was no one else," he went on, in a lighter tone. "Have you then decided to take the veil?"

"Richard!" She looked up, in laughing protest. "Oh, I beg your pardon, sir!"

"There is no need for you to beg my pardon," he answered. "By all means, Richard—I hope to hear you say the name often hereafter. Very well, then, Jane, since you are not destined for a nunnery, what are these reasons of which you spoke?"

His smile was mocking, but Jane could feel the intensity that lay under it, and she shivered a little with emotion. There could be only one outcome now of this interview, she knew, yet, perversely, she sought to delay it.

"I will not be bullied, sir," she said, rallying her forces to speak lightly. "You could hardly expect me to welcome a marriage of convenience."

"But if it were not convenience," he said quickly, taking her hands in his. "If I were to say to you, as I do now—Jane Tarrant, I love you; I loved you when we were here in this inn before; I loved you when we met in Town, though I did not then know it; I loved you even in my dreams, and shall continue to love you for the rest of my life—how if I should say that, Jane?"

Her hands trembled in his. His dark eyes sought hers, but still she kept her head bent.

"What have you to say to that, my lovely Jane?" he insisted. "Could it be possible that this might alter your decision—that you might find it in your heart to love me a little in return?"

She looked up at last, and his pulses leapt at what he saw in her eyes.

"Oh, Richard!" she said, with a little laughing sob in her voice. "Don't you realise that I loved you almost from the first moment? That is the real reason why I could not return the box to you—I was afraid you must see—"

This time she did sway forward, and he caught her in his arms as though he would never let her go again. He bent his face to hers, and stopped her words with his lips.

A log stirred in the fire; its leaping flame outlined the two figures against the dark window, and caught the bright glint of the jewels in the snuff box which lay unregarded on the seat beside them.

THE END

WOMEN OF STRENGTH, PASSION AND BEAUTY... AND THE MEN WHO COULDN'T TAME THEM